P9-EEK-017

THE TRAGEDY OF ROMEO AND JULIET

William Shakespeare

Edited by John R. Hankins

SCHOLASTIC INC.
New York Toronto London Auckland Sydney

ISBN 0-590-41864-5

15 14 13 12 11 10 9   3 4 5/9

Printed in the U.S.A.   01

A WORD TO THE READER

A story of two young lovers caught in the crossfire of a senseless family feud, *The Tragedy of Romeo and Juliet* is Shakespeare's comment on the "generation gap." The teenage lovers and their parents don't seem to understand each other at all. In fact, they don't even communicate. Juliet's father doesn't ask her if she wants to be married. He treats her like a piece of property, something to be handed over to the highest bidder. Romeo never asks his parents for help when he gets into trouble. He turns instead to an understanding outsider — Friar Laurence.

Shakespeare was about 30 years old when he wrote *Romeo and Juliet*, but his sympathies were with the young and loving. The foolish pride and senseless hatred that keeps the feud blazing between the Montagues and Capulets seems to have angered and disgusted him. He puts these feelings into Mercutio's dying words: "A plague on both your houses!"

The story of Romeo and Juliet was popular long before Shakespeare turned it into a play. He borrowed the plot and characters from "The Tragicall Historye of Romeus and Juliet," a long poem written in 1562 by Arthur Brooke. Brooke himself had gotten the idea for his poem from an old Italian story. By literary standards, the poem wasn't very good, but Shakespeare took the germ of the plot and transformed it. His play was published in 1597. It proved to be a "crowd-pleaser," and has since been — in one Elizabethan's words — performed "often with great applause."

For hundreds of years, Romeo and Juliet have been the world's most famous teenagers. Their story has not only enchanted playgoers, but has also been adapted into several film versions. *West Side Story*, one such version, took Romeo and Juliet out of medieval Verona and brought them up-to-date in a New York City ghetto. Director Franco Zeffirelli's new film, however, returns the lovers to 15th-century Verona and has the roles — for the first time in a movie — enacted by teenagers, 17-year-old Leonard Whiting and 15-year-old Olivia Hussey. With young stars in young roles, Shakespeare's play zooms into focus and becomes as timely as today.

The Story

The time is the 15th century. The place is Verona, Italy. The Montagues and the Capulets, two noble families, have long disturbed the city's peace with their senseless feud. The Prince of Verona warns them that the next one to start a fight will be banished or put to death.

At their home, the Capulets are preparing for a masked ball to celebrate the forthcoming marriage of 14-year-old Juliet Capulet to Count Paris. In a spirit of mischief, Romeo Montague crashes the Capulet party with his friend Mercutio. When he sees Juliet there, he falls desperately in love. Juliet returns his feelings, and the two speak of their love in the play's famous balcony scene. Although their parents do not know that they have even met, they plan to marry.

The next morning, Friar Laurence performs the secret marriage ceremony. He hopes that the wedding will end the hatred between the Montagues and the Capulets. After the wedding, Juliet returns home.

Meanwhile, Tybalt (Juliet's cousin) has provoked a quarrel in the street with Mercutio. He jeers at Romeo as the young Montague leaves the church. Mercutio rushes to Romeo's defense with a rapier, and the fight begins.

Horrified, Romeo tries to jump between the two, but Tybalt runs Mercutio through with his sword, killing him. Blind with fury, Romeo duels with Tybalt and kills him. The Prince of Verona banishes Romeo in punishment for his crime. He has only one night to spend with his new bride.

The next morning, Juliet's father insists that she marry Count Paris. Frantic, Juliet begs Friar Laurence for help. He gives her a potion that will cause her to fall into a deathlike coma. Later, when she awakens in the Capulet burial vault, he plans to spirit her away to Romeo.

Romeo fails to receive the friar's message, telling him of the plan. Thinking Juliet is really dead, he buys a vial of poison and hastens to the Capulet tomb. There he takes his last farewell of his bride and drinks the poison.

Waking from her coma, Juliet sees Romeo's dead body. Snatching the dagger from his belt, she kills herself. The death of the lovers brings the Capulets and the Montagues to their senses. Grief-stricken, they finally make peace.

Turning the Play into a Film

Shakespeare wrote his plays more for the ear than
for the eye. The soaring poetry of his lines enabled
Elizabethan audiences to look at an almost bare stage
and imagine the settings that the Bard described. A
movie, however, is made to appeal to the eye. It must
show in order to tell. The moviemaker tries to show
us what is happening (and sometimes *why* it is happening) by using action, images, settings, costumes,
etc.

In his new film version of *Romeo and Juliet*, Franco
Zeffirelli uses visual images to amplify and enhance
Shakespeare's lines. For example, he opens the film
by showing us a hot dusty street teeming with people.
It is a small town where well-to-do young people might
be idle and bored. We see the boredom erupting into
fights, and we see the summer heat igniting tempers.
The scene is set for the bloodshed to come.

Time is short in the play. The action happens in a
matter of days: The lovers meet, marry, and die in less
than a week. The hot summer scene Zeffirelli shows us
gives us a clue as to one of the play's themes. In such
heat, flowers burst into bloom and fade quickly — and
so does love. Verona is a kind of "hot house" for the
lovers. The motion picture camera, with its rapid
movement of frames, makes us feel this atmosphere
of urgent haste.

The action flows swiftly in *Romeo and Juliet*. On
the stage, the frequent breaks between acts — the
opening and closing of the curtains — can slow this
swift flow. A moviemaker need not break a film up
into acts. He can keep things happening without in-
terruption.

To convey the swift pressure of time which is so important to the events in *Romeo and Juliet*, Zeffirelli has taken some liberties with Shakespeare. In the play we see Juliet take the potion. Then we watch the Capulets fussing over her wedding plans before they discover her seemingly lifeless body. Zeffirelli has eliminated the wedding plans and focused instead upon the courtyard of the Capulet house to let the changing light of night to dawn tell us that time has passed. We see the light paling only for a minute, but it is such an eerie, silent light, so full of foreboding that we know some dreadful discovery is about to be made.

Zeffirelli has also cut out the murder of Paris by Romeo. In the play Romeo discovers Paris in the tomb — and kills him, believing he's a prowler. It's the sort of thing that could happen — but must it? Franco Zeffirelli thought not, and in his film there are no distractions for Romeo once he enters the tomb. The camera makes it plain that the only other presence to keep the doomed lovers company is Death.

The Characters

When we meet Romeo, he is a love-lorn youth. He moons about his unrequited affection for a local girl, and Mercutio makes fun of him. But when Romeo falls in love with Juliet, he seems to grow up suddenly. He wants to assume the responsibility of a marriage. He offers friendship to his enemy, Tybalt, and he defends Juliet's Nurse against the gibes and taunts of Mercutio. But Romeo's faults are his undoing. In spite of the goodness of his nature, he is too impatient and hot-tempered. He acts without stopping to think things out, and his impulses bring tragedy.

Loving Romeo has a maturing effect on Juliet. She

is only a child when the play begins, but she meets
the challenge of love wholeheartedly. When she loses
Romeo, she is brave and determined. Even the terrors
of the tomb cannot quench her spirit, for she toasts
Romeo before drinking the potion.

Shakespeare uses comedy to enhance his tragedy in
the characters of Mercutio and the Nurse. Mercutio
is a comedian on purpose, a show-off who likes to
entertain others. The Nurse, however, can't imagine
why people laugh at her. She is proud, stubborn, and
so outspoken that others find her comic. Mercutio's
and the Nurse's bawdy humor heighten the romantic
purity of the lovers.

The minor characters are interesting, too. Tybalt is
a stupid bully and troublemaker, but Lady Capulet is
fond of him. In fact he seems to be the only person
she is fond of, and she shows more emotion at his
death than at Juliet's. Lord Capulet, on the other
hand, is emotional about everything. He fusses and
fumes because he is unsure of himself.

The Meaning

In *Romeo and Juliet,* youth and love are defeated
by hatred and misunderstanding. The lovers are also
defeated by time. They are on a dead run from the
moment they meet each other, for they have only four
days to spend before death closes the play. They have
no time to reconcile their families, or even to escape
by running away together. For them it is always too
late.

Over their short-lived love flickers the impermanence
of light. Juliet compares Romeo's declaration of love
to summer lightning. Her presence seems to him to
shine like the rising sun. They are forced to part when

"Night's candles are burnt out." Their love blazes briefly and is extinguished in the tomb.

The running out of time, the blotting out of day by eternal night — these are two of Shakespeare's themes. He seems to be urging us to love one another, understand one another, before it is too late. Make each moment count, for it will never come again. "Everything that grows," he wrote, "holds in perfection but a little moment." His words might serve as an epitaph for Romeo and Juliet.

— *Margaret Ronan*

Note on the text: This edition follows the text of the second quarto of 1599 (thought to have been printed from Shakespeare's draft) as edited for the Pelican Shakespeare series in 1960. Footnotes are from the Pelican Shakespeare edition.

THE TRAGEDY OF
ROMEO AND JULIET

NAMES OF THE ACTORS

Chorus
Escalus, Prince of Verona
Paris, a young count, kinsman to the Prince
Montague
Capulet
An old Man, of the Capulet family
Romeo, son to Montague
Mercutio, kinsman to the Prince, and friend to Romeo
Benvolio, nephew to Montague, and friend to Romeo
Tybalt, nephew to Lady Capulet
Friar Laurence } Franciscans
Friar John
Balthasar, servant to Romeo
Abram, servant to Montague
Sampson } servants to Capulet
Gregory
Peter, servant to Juliet's nurse
An Apothecary
Three Musicians
An Officer
Lady Montague, wife to Montague
Lady Capulet, wife to Capulet
Juliet, daughter to Capulet
Nurse to Juliet
Citizens of Verona, Gentlemen and Gentlewomen of
    both houses, Maskers, Torchbearers, Pages, Guards,
    Watchmen, Servants, and Attendants

SCENE

Verona, Mantua

THE PROLOGUE

Enter Chorus.

Chorus. Two households, both alike in dignity,
    In fair Verona, where we lay our scene,
From ancient grudge break to new mutiny,
    Where civil blood makes civil hands unclean.
From forth the fatal loins of these two foes   5
    A pair of star-crossed lovers take their life;
Whose misadventured piteous overthrows
    Doth with their death bury their parents' strife.
The fearful passage of their death-marked love,
    And the continuance of their parents' rage,   10
Which, but their children's end, naught could
      remove,
    Is now the two hours' traffic of our stage;
The which if you with patient ears attend,
What here shall miss, our toil shall strive to mend.
    Exit.

Pro., 3 *mutiny* outbursts of violence 4 *civil . . . civil* citizens' . . .
fellow citizens' 6 *star-crossed* thwarted by adverse stars 9 *death-marked* foredoomed to death 12 *two . . . stage* our stage-business
for the next two hours

ACT I, SCENE I

Enter Sampson and Gregory, with swords and bucklers, of the house of Capulet.

Sampson. Gregory, on my word, we'll not carry coals.
Gregory. No, for then we shall be colliers.
Sampson. I mean, an we be in choler, we'll draw.
Gregory. Ay, while you live, draw your neck out of
5   collar.
Sampson. I strike quickly, being moved.
Gregory. But thou art not quickly moved to strike.
Sampson. A dog of the house of Montague moves me.
Gregory. To move is to stir, and to be valiant is to
10   stand.
      Therefore, if thou art moved, thou runn'st away.
Sampson. A dog of that house shall move me to
      stand. I will take the wall of any man or maid of
      Montague's.
15 *Gregory.* That shows thee a weak slave; for the weakest
      goes to the wall.
Sampson. 'Tis true; and therefore women, being the
      weaker vessels, are ever thrust to the wall. Therefore
      I will push Montague's men from the wall and
20   thrust his maids to the wall.
Gregory. The quarrel is between our masters, and us
      their men.
Sampson. 'Tis all one. I will show myself a tyrant.
      When I have fought with the men, I will be cruel
25   with the maids—I will cut off their heads.
Gregory. The heads of the maids?
Sampson. Ay, the heads of the maids, or their maiden-
      heads. Take it in what sense thou wilt.
Gregory. They must take it in sense that feel it.

I, i, 1 *carry coals* i.e. suffer insults 2 *colliers* coal dealers 3 *an* if
choler anger *draw* draw our swords 5 *collar* hangman's noose
13 *take the wall* pass on the inner and cleaner part of the side-
walk 15–16 *the weakest . . . wall* i.e. is pushed from his place
(proverbial) 18 *weaker vessels* (cf. 1 Peter 3:7) 28–29 *sense . . .
sense* meaning . . . physical sensation

Sampson. Me they shall feel while I am able to stand;   30
and 'tis known I am a pretty piece of flesh.

Gregory. 'Tis well thou art not fish; if thou hadst, thou
hadst been poor-John. Draw thy tool! Here comes
two of the house of Montagues.

Enter two other Servingmen (Abram and Balthasar)

Sampson. My naked weapon is out. Quarrel! I will   35
back thee.

Gregory. How? turn thy back and run?

Sampson. Fear me not.

Gregory. No, marry. I fear thee!

Sampson. Let us take the law of our sides; let them   40
begin.

Gregory. I will frown as I pass by, and let them take it
as they list.

Sampson. Nay, as they dare. I will bite my thumb at
them, which is disgrace to them if they bear it.   45

Abram. Do you bite your thumb at us, sir?

Sampson. I do bite my thumb, sir.

Abram. Do you bite your thumb at us, sir?

Sampson. (*aside to Gregory*) Is the law of our side if I
say ay?   50

Gregory. (*aside to Sampson*) No.

Sampson. No, sir, I do not bite my thumb at you, sir;
but I bite my thumb, sir.

Gregory. Do you quarrel, sir?

Abram. Quarrel, sir? No, sir.   55

Sampson. But if you do, sir, I am for you. I serve as
good a man as you.

Abram. No better.

Sampson. Well, sir.

31, 32 *flesh, fish* alluding to the proverb "Neither fish nor flesh'
33 *poor-John* dried hake, the cheapest fish *tool* sword 39 *marry*
indeed (originally an oath by the Virgin Mary) *I fear thee* to
suppose me afraid of you is ridiculous 40 *take . . . of* have the
law on 44 *bite my thumb* an insulting gesture

Enter Benvolio.

60 *Gregory. (aside to Sampson)* Say "better." Here comes
      one of my master's kinsmen.
    Sampson. Yes, better, sir.
    Abram. You lie.
    Sampson. Draw, if you be men. Gregory, remember thy
65   swashing blow.   *They fight.*
    Benvolio. Part, fools!
      Put up your swords. You know not what you do.

Enter Tybalt.

    Tybalt. What, art thou drawn among these heartless
      hinds? Turn thee, Benvolio! look upon thy death.
70 *Benvolio.* I do but keep the peace. Put up thy sword,
      Or manage it to part these men with me.
    Tybalt. What, drawn, and talk of peace? I hate the
      word as I hate hell, all Montagues, and thee.
      Have at thee, coward!   *They fight.*

*Enter an Officer and three or four Citizens with clubs
or partisans.*

75 *Officer.* Clubs, bills, and partisans! Strike! beat them
      down!
    Citizens. Down with the Capulets! Down with the
      Montagues!

Enter old Capulet in his gown and Lady Capulet.

    Capulet. What noise is this? Give me my long sword,
80   ho!

---

65 *swashing* smashing 68–69 *heartless hinds* cowardly servants 75
bills, partisans long-shafted weapons with combined spearhead and
cutting-blade

Lady. A crutch, a crutch! Why call you for a sword?
Capulet. My sword, I say! Old Montague is come
And flourishes his blade in spite of me.

Enter old Montague and Lady Montague

Montague. Thou villain Capulet! — Hold me not, let
me go.   85
Lady. Thou shalt not stir one foot to seek a foe.

Enter Prince Escalus, with his train.

Prince. Rebellious subjects, enemies to peace,
Profaners of this neighbor-stainèd steel —
Will they not hear? What, ho! you men, you beasts,
That quench the fire of your pernicious rage   90
With purple fountains issuing from your veins!
On pain of torture, from those bloody hands
Throw your mistemperèd weapons to the ground
And hear the sentence of your movèd prince.
Three civil brawls, bred of an airy word   95
By thee, old Capulet, and Montague,
Have thrice disturbed the quiet of our streets
And made Verona's ancient citizens
Cast by their grave beseeming ornaments
To wield old partisans, in hands as old,   100
Cank'red with peace, to part your cank'red hate.
If ever you disturb our streets again,
Your lives shall pay the forfeit of the peace.
For this time all the rest depart away.
You Capulet, shall go along with me;   105

83 *in spite of* in defiance of 93 *mistemperèd* (1) badly made (2)
used for a bad purpose 95 *airy* made with breath 98 *ancient citizens* a volunteer guard of older men 99 *grave beseeming ornaments*
staffs and costumes appropriate for the aged 101 *Cank'red . . .
cank'red* rusted . . . malignant

And, Montague, come you this afternoon,
To know our farther pleasure in this case,
To old Freetown, our common judgment place.
Once more, on pain of death, all men depart.

Exit all but Montague, Lady Montague, and Benvolio.

110 *Montague.* Who set this ancient quarrel new abroach?
Speak, nephew, were you by when it began?
Benvolio. Here were the servants of your adversary
And yours, close fighting ere I did approach.
I drew to part them. In the instant came
115 The fiery Tybalt, with his sword prepared;
Which, as he breathed defiance to my ears,
He swung about his head and cut the winds,
Who, nothing hurt withal, hissed him in scorn.
While we were interchanging thrusts and blows,
120 Came more and more, and fought on part and part,
Till the Prince came, who parted either part.
Lady. O, where is Romeo? Saw you him today?
Right glad I am he was not at this fray.
Benvolio. Madam, an hour before the worshipped sun
125 Peered forth the golden window of the East,
A troubled mind drave me to walk abroad;
Where, underneath the grove of sycamore
That westward rooteth from this city side,
So early walking did I see your son.
130 Towards him I made, but he was ware of me
And stole into the covert of the wood.
I, measuring his affections by my own,
Which then most sought where most might not
be found,

110 *set . . . abroach* reopened this quarrel of long standing 118
Who which *nothing* not at all *withal* therewith 130 *ware* aware,
wary 132 *affections* inclinations, feelings 133 *most sought . . .
found* i.e. desired solitude

Being one too many by my weary self,
Pursued my humor, not pursuing his,   135
And gladly shunned who gladly fled from me.
Montague. Many a morning hath he there been seen,
  With tears augmenting the fresh morning's dew,
  Adding to clouds more clouds with his deep sighs;
  But all so soon as the all-cheering sun   140
  Should in the farthest East begin to draw
  The shady curtains from Aurora's bed,
  Away from light steals home my heavy son
  And private in his chamber pens himself,
  Shuts up his windows, locks fair daylight out,   145
  And makes himself an artificial night.
  Black and portentous must this humor prove
  Unless good counsel may the cause remove.
Benvolio. My noble uncle, do you know the cause?
Montague. I neither know it nor can learn of him.   150
Benvolio. Have you importuned him by any means?
Montague. Both by myself and many other friends;
  But he, his own affections' counsellor,
  Is to himself — I will not say how true —
  But to himself so secret and so close,   155
  So far from sounding and discovery,
  As is the bud bit with an envious worm
  Ere he can spread his sweet leaves to the air
  Or dedicate his beauty to the sun.
  Could we but learn from whence his sorrows grow,   160
  We would as willingly give cure as know.

Enter Romeo.

Benvolio. See, where he comes. So please you step
  aside,
  I'll know his grievance, or be much denied.

142 *Aurora* the dawn 143 *heavy* melancholy 147 *humor* mood
156 *sounding* being measured (as water-depth is measured with a
plummet line)

Montague. I would thou wert so happy by thy stay
165 To hear true shrift. Come, madam, let's away.

Exit Montague and Lady Montague.

Benvolio. Good morrow, cousin.
Romeo.   Is the day so young?
Benvolio. But new struck nine.
Romeo.   Ay me! sad hours seem long.
  Was that my father that went hence so fast?
Benvolio. It was. What sadness lengthens Romeo's
  hours?
Romeo. Not having that which having makes them
170 short.
Benvolio. In love?
Romeo. Out —
Benvolio. Of love?
Romeo. Out of her favor where I am in love.
175 *Benvolio.* Alas that love, so gentle in his view,
  Should be so tyrannous and rough in proof!
Romeo. Alas that love, whose view is muffled still,
  Should without eyes see pathways to his will!
  Where shall we dine? O me! What fray was here?
180 Yet tell me not, for I have heard it all.
  Here's much to do with hate, but more with love.
  Why then, O brawling love, O loving hate,
  O anything, of nothing first create!
  O heavy lightness, serious vanity,
185 Misshapen chaos of well-seeming forms,
  Feather of lead, bright smoke, cold fire, sick health,
  Still-waking sleep, that is not what it is!
  This love feel I, that feel no love in this.
  Dost thou not laugh?

---

165 *shrift* confession 166 *morrow* morning 175 *view* appearance
176 *in proof* in being experienced 177 *view* sight *muffled* blindfolded

Benvolio.   No, coz, I rather weep.
Romeo. Good heart, at what?
Benvolio.   At thy good heart's oppression.   190
Romeo. Why, such is love's transgression.
   Griefs of mine own lie heavy in my breast,
   Which thou wilt propagate, to have it prest
   With more of thine. This love that thou hast shown
   Doth add more grief to too much of mine own.   195
   Love is a smoke raised with the fume of sighs;
   Being purged, a fire sparkling in lovers' eyes;
   Being vexed, a sea nourished with lovers' tears.
   What is it else? A madness most discreet,
   A choking gall, and a preserving sweet.   200
   Farewell, my coz.
Benvolio.   Soft! I will go along.
   An if you leave me so, you do me wrong.
Romeo. Tut! I have lost myself; I am not here;
   This is not Romeo, he's some other where.
Benvolio. Tell me in sadness, who is that you love?   205
Romeo. What, shall I groan and tell thee?
Benvolio.   Groan? Why, no;
   But sadly tell me who.
Romeo. Bid a sick man in sadness make his will.
   Ah, word ill urged to one that is so ill!
   In sadness, cousin, I do love a woman.   210
Benvolio. I aimed so near when I supposed you loved.
Romeo. A right good markman. And she's fair I love.
Benvolio. A right fair mark, fair coz, is soonest hit.
Romeo. Well, in that hit you miss. She'll not be hit
   With Cupid's arrow. She hath Dian's wit,   215
   And, in strong proof of chastity well armed,
   From Love's weak childish bow she lives unharmed.

---

189 *coz* cousin   192 *Griefs . . . own* your sorrow for my grief grieves
me further to have caused you sorrow   205 *in sadness* seriously   213
fair mark bright clean target   215 *Dian* Diana, virgin goddess and
huntress

She will not stay the siege of loving terms,
Nor bide th' encounter of assailing eyes,
220 Nor ope her lap to saint-seducing gold.
O, she is rich in beauty; only poor
That, when she dies, with beauty dies her store.

Benvolio. Then she hath sworn that she will still live
chaste?

Romeo. She hath, and in that sparing makes huge
waste;
225 For beauty, starved with her severity,
Cuts beauty off from all posterity.
She is too fair, too wise, wisely too fair,
To merit bliss by making me despair.
She hath forsworn to love, and in that vow
230 Do I live dead that live to tell it now.

Benvolio. Be ruled by me; forget to think of her.

Romeo. O, teach me how I should forget to think!

Benvolio. By giving liberty unto thine eyes.
Examine other beauties.

Romeo.   'Tis the way
235 To call hers (exquisite) in question more.
These happy masks that kiss fair ladies' brows,
Being black puts us in mind they hide the fair.
He that is strucken blind cannot forget
The precious treasure of his eyesight lost.
240 Show me a mistress that is passing fair,
What doth her beauty serve but as a note
Where I may read who passed that passing fair?
Farewell. Thou canst not teach me to forget.

Benvolio. I'll pay that doctrine, or else die in debt. *Exit.*

---

216 *proof* armor   218–219 *She . . . eyes* i.e. she gives me no chance
to woo her   222 *with . . . store* she will leave no children to per-
petuate her beauty   223 *still* always   224 *sparing* miserly economy
228 *bliss* heaven   235 *in question* to my mind   240 *passing* sur-
passingly   244 *pay that doctrine* convince you otherwise

ACT I, SCENE II

Enter Capulet, County Paris, and the Clown (a Servant).

Capulet. But Montague is bound as well as I,
    In penalty alike; and 'tis not hard, I think,
    For men so old as we to keep the peace.
Paris. Of honorable reckoning are you both,
    And pity 'tis you lived at odds so long.   5
    But now, my lord, what say you to my suit?
Capulet. But saying o'er what I have said before:
    My child is yet a stranger in the world,
    She hath not seen the change of fourteen years;
    Let two more summers wither in their pride   10
    Ere we may think her ripe to be a bride.
Paris. Younger than she are happy mothers made.
Capulet. And too soon marred are those so early made.
    The earth hath swallowèd all my hopes but she;
    She is the hopeful lady of my earth.   15
    But woo her, gentle Paris, get her heart;
    My will to her consent is but a part.
    An she agree, within her scope of choice
    Lies my consent and fair according voice.
    This night I hold an old accustomed feast,   20
    Whereto I have invited many a guest,
    Such as I love; and you among the store,
    One more, most welcome, makes my number more.
    At my poor house look to behold this night
    Earth-treading stars that make dark heaven light.   25
    Such comfort as do lusty young men feel
    When well-apparelled April on the heel
    Of limping Winter treads, even such delight
    Among fresh fennel buds shall you this night

I, ii, 1 *bound* under bond 4 *reckoning* reputation 8 *world* world of society 14 *hopes* children 18 *scope* range 19 *according* harmoniously agreeing 20 *old accustomed* by custom of long standing 25 *stars* i.e. maidens 27 *April* Venus' month, the season of love 29 *fennel* a flowering herb associated with enticement

30   Inherit at my house. Hear all, all see,
        And like her most whose merit most shall be;
        Which, on more view of many, mine, being one,
        May stand in number, though in reck'ning none.
        Come, go with me. *(to Servant, giving him a paper)*
          Go, sirrah, trudge about
35   Through fair Verona; find those persons out
        Whose names are written there, and to them say,
        My house and welcome on their pleasure stay.
                                        Exit (with Paris).
Servant. Find them out whose names are written here?
        It is written that the shoemaker should meddle with
40   his yard and the tailor with his last, the fisher with
        his pencil and the painter with his nets; but I am sent
        to find those persons whose names are here writ, and
        can never find what names the writing person hath
        here writ. I must to the learned. In good time!

                    Enter Benvolio and Romeo.

45 *Benvolio.* Tut, man, one fire burns out another's burn-
          ing;
          One pain is less'ned by another's anguish;
        Turn giddy, and be holp by backward turning;
          One desperate grief cures with another's languish.
        Take thou some new infection to thy eye,
50   And the rank poison of the old will die.
    Romeo. Your plantain leaf is excellent for that.
    Benvolio. For what, I pray thee?
    Romeo.   For your broken shin.

32–33 *Which . . . none* my daughter will be numerically counted
among those present, but possibly not among those you would wish
to marry after seeing them all 34 *sirrah* a familiar form of address, used with servants and sometimes with friends 40–41 *yard,
last, pencil, nets* occupational tools humorously reversed 42 *find*
find out (since I cannot read) 44 *In good time* help comes just
when I need it 45 *one . . . burning* proverb used often by Shakespeare 46 *another's anguish* anguish from another pain 47 *Turn
. . . turning* when giddy from whirling around, be helped by re-
versing direction 49 *infection* figuratively used, but taken literally
by Romeo

Benvolio. Why, Romeo, art thou mad?

Romeo. Not mad, but bound more than a madman is;
    Shut up in prison, kept without my food,   55
    Whipped and tormented and — God-den, good
      fellow.

Servant. God gi' go-den. I pray, sir, can you read?

Romeo. Ay, mine own fortune in my misery.

Servant. Perhaps you have learned it without book.
    But I pray, can you read anything you see?   60

Romeo. Ay, if I know the letters and the language.

Servant. Ye say honestly. Rest you merry.

Romeo. Stay, fellow; I can read.   *He reads the letter.*
    "Signior Martino and his wife and daughters;
    County Anselmo and his beauteous sisters;   65
    The lady widow of Vitruvio;
    Signior Placentio and his lovely nieces;
    Mercutio and his brother Valentine;
    Mine uncle Capulet, his wife, and daughters;
    My fair niece Rosaline and Livia;   70
    Signior Valentio and his cousin Tybalt;
    Lucio and the lively Helena."
    A fair assembly. Whither should they come?

Servant. Up.

Romeo. Whither? To supper?   75

Servant. To our house.

Romeo. Whose house?

Servant. My master's.

Romeo. Indeed I should have asked you that before.

Servant. Now I'll tell you without asking. My master is   80
    the great rich Capulet; and if you be not of the house
    of Montagues, I pray come and crush a cup of wine.
    Rest you merry.   *Exit.*

54–56 *bound . . . tormented* customary treatment of madmen 56
God-den good evening used after 12:00 noon 61 *if I know* the
servant takes this to mean "only if I have memorized the appearance
of" 82 *crush* drink

Benvolio. At this same ancient feast of Capulet's
85   Sups the fair Rosaline whom thou so loves;
      With all the admirèd beauties of Verona.
      Go thither, and with unattainted eye
      Compare her face with some that I shall show,
      And I will make thee think thy swan a crow.
90 *Romeo.* When the devout religion of mine eye
        Maintains such falsehood, then turn tears to fires;
      And these, who, often drowned, could never die,
        Transparent heretics, be burnt for liars!
      One fairer than my love? The all-seeing sun
95   Ne'er saw her match since first the world begun.
Benvolio. Tut! you saw her fair, none else being by,
      Herself poised with herself in either eye;
      But in that crystal scales let there be weighed
      Your lady's love against some other maid
100   That I will show you shining at this feast,
      And she shall scant show well that now seems best.
Romeo. I'll go along, no such sight to be shown,
      But to rejoice in splendor of my own.   *Exit.*

ACT I, SCENE III

Enter Lady Capulet and Nurse.

Lady. Nurse, where's my daughter? Call her forth to
    me.
Nurse. Now, by my maidenhead at twelve year old,

---

87 *unattainted* unprejudiced 92 *these* these eyes *drowned* i.e. in
tears 98 *crystal scales* Romeo's two eyes are compared to the two
ends of a pair of balancès 101 *scant* scarcely

I bade her come. What, lamb! what, ladybird!
God forbid, where's this girl? What, Juliet!

Enter Juliet.

Juliet. How now? Who calls?
Nurse.   Your mother.
Juliet.   Madame, I am here.   5
  What is your will?
Lady. This is the matter —. Nurse, give leave awhile,
  We must talk in secret. Nurse, come back again;
  I have rememb'red me, thou's hear our counsel.
  Thou knowest my daughter's of a pretty age.   10
Nurse. Faith, I can tell her age unto an hour.
Lady. She's not fourteen.
Nurse.   I'll lay fourteen of my teeth —
  And yet, to my teen be it spoken, I have but four —
  She's not fourteen. How long is it now
  To Lammastide?
Lady.   A fortnight and odd days.   15
Nurse. Even or odd, of all days in the year,
  Come Lammas Eve at night shall she be fourteen.
  Susan and she (God rest all Christian souls!)
  Were of an age. Well, Susan is with God;
  She was too good for me. But, as I said,   20
  On Lammas Eve at night shall she be fourteen;
  That shall she, marry; I remember it well.
  'Tis since the earthquake now eleven years;
  And she was weaned (I never shall forget it),
  Of all the days of the year, upon that day;   25
  For I had then laid wormwood to my dug,
  Sitting in the sun under the dovehouse wall.

I, iii. 7 *give leave* leave us   9 *thou's* thou shalt   13 *teen* sorrow
15 *Lammastide* August 1st

My lord and you were then at Mantua.
Nay, I do bear a brain. But, as I said,
30 When it did taste the wormwood on the nipple
Of my dug and felt it bitter, pretty fool,
To see it tetchy and fall out with the dug!
Shake, quoth the dovehouse! 'Twas no need, I trow,
To bid me trudge.
35 And since that time it is eleven years,
For then she could stand high-lone; nay, by th' rood,
She could have run and waddled all about;
For even the day before, she broke her brow;
And then my husband (God be with his soul!
40 'A was a merry man) took up the child.
"Yea," quoth he, "dost thou fall upon thy face?
Thou wilt fall backward when thou hast more wit;
Wilt thou not, Jule?" and, by my holidam,
The pretty wretch left crying and said "Ay."
45 To see now how a jest shall come about!
I warrant, an I should live a thousand years,
I never should forget it. "Wilt thou not, Jule?"
     quoth he,
And, pretty fool, it stinted and said "Ay."
Lady. Enough of this. I pray thee hold thy peace.
50 *Nurse.* Yes, madam. Yet I cannot choose but laugh
To think it should leave crying and say "Ay."
And yet, I warrant, it had upon it brow
A bump as big as a young cock'rel's stone;
A perilous knock; and it cried bitterly.
55 "Yea," quoth my husband, "fall'st upon thy face?
Thou wilt fall backward when thou comest to age;
Wilt thou not, Jule?" It stinted and said "Ay."
Juliet. And stint thou too, I pray thee, nurse, say I.

29 *bear a brain* keep my mental powers 32 *tetchy* fretful 33
Shakes . . . dovehouse i.e. the dovehouse creaked from the earthquake *trow* believe 34 *trudge* run away 36 *high-lone* alone *rood*
cross 43 *holidam* halidom, holy relic 48 *stinted* stopped 52 *it brow*
its brow 58 *say I* a pun on "ay" and "I"

Nurse. Peace, I have done. God mark thee to his grace!
    Thou wast the prettiest babe that e'er I nursed.   60
    An I might live to see thee married once,
    I have my wish.
Lady. Marry, that "marry" is the very theme
    I came to talk of. Tell me, daughter Juliet,
    How stands your disposition to be married?   65
Juliet. It is an honor that I dream not of.
Nurse. An honor? Were not I thine only nurse,
    I would say thou hadst sucked wisdom from thy teat.
Lady. Well, think of marriage now. Younger than you,
    Here in Verona, ladies of esteem,   70
    Are made already mothers. By my count,
    I was your mother much upon these years
    That you are now a maid. Thus then in brief:
    The valiant Paris seeks you for his love.
Nurse. A man, young lady! lady, such a man   75
    As all the world — why he's a man of wax.
Lady. Verona's summer hath not such a flower.
Nurse. Nay, he's a flower, in faith — a very flower.
Lady. What say you? Can you love the gentleman?
    This night you shall behold him at our feast.   80
    Read o'er the volume of young Paris' face,
    And find delight writ there with beauty's pen;
    Examine every married lineament,
    And see how one another lends content;
    And what obscured in this fair volume lies   85
    Find written in the margent of his eyes.
    This precious book of love, this unbound lover,
    To beautify him only lacks a cover.

---

72 *much . . . years* at much the same age (indicating that Lady
Capulet's age is now twenty-eight) 76 *a man of wax* handsome, as
a wax model 83 *married lineament* harmonious feature 85 *what
. . . lies* i.e. his concealed inner qualities of character 86 *margent*
marginal gloss 88 *a cover* i.e. a wife

The fish lives in the sea, and 'tis much pride
90   For fair without the fair within to hide.
That book in many's eyes doth share the glory,
That in gold clasps locks in the golden story;
So shall you share all that he doth possess,
By having him making yourself no less.
95 *Nurse.* No less? Nay, bigger! Women grow by men.
Lady. Speak briefly, can you like of Paris' love?
Juliet. I'll look to like, if looking liking move;
But no more deep will I endart mine eye
Than your consent gives strength to make it fly.

Enter Servingman.

100 *Servingman.* Madam, the guests are come, supper
served up, you called, my young lady asked for, the
nurse cursed in the pantry, and everything in ex-
tremity. I must hence to wait. I beseech you follow
straight.
Lady. We follow thee. (*Exit Servingman.*) Juliet, the
105   County stays.
Nurse. Go, girl, seek happy nights to happy days.
                                                Exit.

89–94 *The fish . . . no less* i.e. as the sea enfolds the fish and the
cover enfolds the book, so you shall enfold Paris (in your arms),
enhancing your good qualities by sharing his   95 *bigger* i.e. through
pregnancy 98 *endart mine eye* shoot my eye-glance (as an arrow)
102 *cursed in the pantry* i.e. the other servants swear because the
Nurse is not helping 105 *County* referring to Count Paris, obsolete
form of address

ACT I, SCENE IV

Enter Romeo, Mercutio, Benvolio with five or six other Maskers; Torchbearers.

Romeo. What, shall this speech be spoke for our
    excuse?
  Or shall we on without apology?
Benvolio. The date is out of such prolixity.
  We'll have no Cupid hoodwinked with a scarf,
  Bearing a Tartar's painted bow of lath,   5
  Scaring the ladies like a crowkeeper;
  (Nor no without-book prologue, faintly spoke
  After the prompter, for our entrance);
  But, let them measure us by what they will,
  We'll measure them a measure and be gone.   10
Romeo. Give me a torch. I am not for this ambling.
  Being but heavy, I will bear the light.
Mercutio. Nay, gentle Romeo, we must have you dance.
Romeo. Not I, believe me. You have dancing shoes
  With nimble soles; I have a soul of lead   15
  So stakes me to the ground I cannot move.
Mercutio. You are a lover. Borrow Cupid's wings
  And soar with them above a common bound.
Romeo. I am too sore enpiercèd with his shaft
  To soar with his light feathers; and so bound   20

I, iv. 1 *this speech* Romeo has prepared a set speech, such as
customarily introduced visiting maskers 3 *The date . . . prolixity*
such superfluous speeches are now out of fashion 4 *hoodwinked*
blindfolded 5 *Tartar's . . . lath* the Tartar's bow, used from horse-
back, was much shorter than the English longbow 6 *crowkeeper*
scarecrow 7 *without-book* memorized 10 *measure . . . measure*
dance one dance 12 *heavy* sad, hence "weighted down" 18 *bound*
a leap, required in some dances

I cannot bound a pitch above dull woe.
Under love's heavy burden do I sink.

Mercutio. And, to sink in it, should you burden love —
Too great oppression for a tender thing.

25 *Romeo.* Is love a tender thing? It is too rough,
Too rude, too boist'rous, and it pricks like thorn.

Mercutio. If love be rough with you, be rough with
love.
Prick love for pricking, and you beat love down.
Give me a case to put my visage in.

30 A visor for a visor! What care I
What curious eye doth quote deformities?
Here are the beetle brows shall blush for me.

Benvolio. Come, knock and enter; and no sooner in
But every man betake him to his legs.

35 *Romeo.* A torch for me! Let wantons light of heart
Tickle the senseless rushes with their heels;
For I am proverbed with a grandsire phrase,
I'll be a candle-holder and look on;
The game was ne'er so fair, and I am done.

Mercutio. Tut! dun's the mouse, the constable's own
40 word!
If thou art Dun, we'll draw thee from the mire
Of this sir-reverence love, wherein thou stickest
Up to the ears. Come, we burn daylight, ho!

Romeo. Nay, that's not so.

Mercutio.   I mean, sir, in delay
45 We waste our lights in vain, like lamps by day.

21 *pitch* height (falconry) 30 *A visor . . . visor* a mask for a face
ugly enough to be itself a mask 31 *quote* note 32 *beetle brows*
beetling eyebrows (of the mask) 34 *betake . . . legs* join the dance
36 *rushes* used as floor coverings 37 *grandsire phrase* old saying
38 *candle-holder* i.e. nonparticipant 39 *The game . . . done* best
quit a game at the height of enjoyment (proverbial) 40 *dun's
the mouse* be quiet as a mouse (proverbial) *constable's own word*
i.e. the caution to be quiet 41 *Dun* stock name for a horse *mire*
alluding to a winter game, "Dun is in the mire," in which the
players lifted a heavy log representing a horse caught in the mud
42 *sir-reverence* filthy (literally "save-your-reverence," a euphemism
associated with physical functions 43 *burn daylight* waste time
(proverbial)

Take our good meaning, for our judgment sits
Five times in that ere once in our five wits.
Romeo. And we mean well in going to this masque,
But 'tis no wit to go.
Mercutio.   Why, may one ask?
Romeo. I dreamt a dream tonight.
Mercutio.   And so did I.   50
Romeo. Well, what was yours?
Mercutio.   That dreamers often lie.
Romeo. In bed asleep, while they do dream things true.
Mercutio. O, then I see Queen Mab hath been with
    you.
She is the fairies' midwife, and she comes
In shape no bigger than an agate stone   55
On the forefinger of an alderman,
Drawn with a team of little atomies
Over men's noses as they lie asleep;
Her wagon spokes made of long spinners' legs,
The cover, of the wings of grasshoppers;   60
Her traces, of the smallest spider's web;
Her collars, of the moonshine's wat'ry beams;
Her whip, of cricket's bone; the lash, of film;
Her wagoner, a small grey-coated gnat,
Not half so big as a round little worm   65
Pricked from the lazy finger of a maid;
Her chariot is an empty hazelnut,
Made by the joiner squirrel or old grub,
Time out o' mind the fairies' coachmakers.
And in this state she gallops night by night   70
Through lovers' brains, and then they dream of love;
O'er courtiers' knees, that dream on curtsies straight;

---

47 *five wits* mental faculties: common sense (the perceptive power
common to all five physical senses), fantasy, imagination, judgment
(reason), memory   49 *no wit* not intelligent   53 *Mab* a Celtic folk
name for the fairy queen   55 *agate stone* a fine-grained, multicolored
stone   57 *atomies* tiny creatures   59 *spinners* spiders   61, 62 *traces,
collars* parts of the harness   63 *film* filament of a spider's web
65–66 *worm . . . maid* alluding to the proverbial saying that worms
breed in idle fingers

O'er lawyers' fingers, who straight dream on fees;
O'er ladies' lips, who straight on kisses dream,
75 Which oft the angry Mab with blisters plagues,
Because their breaths with sweetmeats tainted are.
Sometime she gallops o'er a courtier's nose,
And then dreams he of smelling out a suit;
And sometime comes she with a tithe-pig's tail
80 Tickling a parson's nose as 'a lies asleep,
Then dreams he of another benefice.
Sometimes she driveth o'er a soldier's neck,
And then dreams he of cutting foreign throats,
Of breaches, ambuscadoes, Spanish blades,
85 Of healths five fathom deep; and then anon
Drums in his ear, at which he starts and wakes,
And being thus frighted, swears a prayer or two
And sleeps again. This is that very Mab
That plaits the manes of horses in the night
90 And bakes the elflocks in foul sluttish hairs,
Which once untangled much misfortune bodes.
This is the hag, when maids lie on their backs,
That presses them and learns them first to bear,
Making them women of good carriage.
This is she —
95 *Romeo.*   Peace, peace, Mercutio, peace!
Thou talk'st of nothing.
Mercutio.   True, I talk of dreams;
Which are the children of an idle brain,
Begot of nothing but vain fantasy;
Which is as thin of substance as the air,
100 And more inconstant than the wind, who woos
Even now the frozen bosom of the North

76 *with sweetmeats* i.e. as a result of eating sweetmeats   78 *smelling
. . . suit* discovering a petitioner who will pay for his influence with
government officials   79 *tithe-pig* the parson's tithe (tenth) of his
parishioner's livestock   81 *another benefice* an additional "living"
in the church   85 *healths . . . deep* drinking toasts from glasses
thirty feet deep   90 *elflocks* knots of tangled hair   92 *hag* night
hag, or nightmare   96 *nothing* no tangible thing

And, being angered, puffs away from thence,
Turning his side to the dew-dropping South.

Benvolio. This wind you talk of blows us from our-
selves.

Supper is done, and we shall come too late.   105

Romeo. I fear, too early; for my mind misgives
Some consequence, yet hanging in the stars,
Shall bitterly begin his fearful date
With this night's revels and expire the term
Of a despisèd life, closed in my breast,   110
By some vile forfeit of untimely death.
But he that hath the steerage of my course
Direct my sail! On, lusty gentlemen!

Benvolio. Strike, drum.

ACT I, SCENE V

*They march about the stage, and Servingmen come forth
with napkins.*

1. *Servingman.* Where's Potpan, that he helps not to
take away? He shift a trencher! he scrape a trencher!

2. *Servingman.* When good manners shall lie all in one
or two men's hands, and they unwashed too, 'tis a
foul thing.   5

1. *Servingman.* Away with the joint-stools, remove the
court-cupboard, look to the plate. Good thou, save

---

107 *consequence* future chain of events *hanging* in astrology, future
events are said to "hang"—*dependere*—from the stars   112 *he* God
I, v,   2 *trencher* wooden platter   3–5 *When . . . thing* a complaint
that household decorum, "good manners," is sustained by too few,
and too untidy, servants   6 *joint-stools* stools made by a joiner

me a piece of marchpane and, as thou loves me, let
the porter let in Susan Grindstone and Nell. (*Exit*
10   *second Servingman.*) Anthony, and Potpan!

Enter two more Servingmen.

3. *Servingman.* Ay, boy, ready.
1. *Servingman.* You are looked for and called for, asked
for and sought for, in the great chamber.
4. *Servingman.* We cannot be here and there too.
15   Cheerly, boys! Be brisk awhile, and the longer liver
take all.

          Exit third and fourth Servingmen.

*Enter Capulet, Lady Capulet, Juliet, Tybalt, Nurse, and
all the Guests and Gentlewomen to the Maskers.*

Capulet. Welcome, gentlemen! Ladies that have their
    toes
Unplagued with corns will walk about with you.
Ah ha, my mistresses! which of you all
20   Will now deny to dance? She that makes dainty,
She I'll swear hath corns. Am I come near ye now?
Welcome, gentlemen! I have seen the day
That I have worn a visor and could tell
A whispering tale in a fair lady's ear,
25   Such as would please. 'Tis gone, 'tis gone, 'tis gone!
You are welcome, gentlemen! Come, musicians,
    play.

        Music plays, and they dance.
A hall, a hall! give room! and foot it, girls.

---

7 *court-cupboard* sideboard *plate* silverware 8 *marchpane* sweet-
meat with almonds 9 *Susan . . . Nell* girls evidently invited for a
servants' party in the kitchen after the banquet 11, 14 3. *Servingman,* 4. *Servingman* presumably they are Anthony and Potpan, now
arrived 15 *longer . . . all* i.e. the spoils to the survivor (proverbial,
but often used in contexts like the above, advocating enjoyment of
life) 18 *walk about* dance a turn 20 *makes dainty* pretends to
hesitate 27 *A hall* clear the hall for dancing

More light, you knaves! and turn the tables up,
And quench the fire, the room is grown too hot.
Ah, sirrah, this unlooked-for sport comes well.   30
Nay, sit, nay, sit, good cousin Capulet,
For you and I are past our dancing days.
How long is't now since last yourself and I
Were in a mask?

2. *Capulet.*   By'r Lady, thirty years.

Capulet. What, man? 'Tis not so much, 'tis not so   35
much; 'Tis since the nuptial of Lucentio,
Come Pentecost as quickly as it will,
Some five-and-twenty years, and then we masked.

2. *Capulet.* 'Tis more, 'tis more. His son is elder, sir;
His son is thirty.

Capulet.   Will you tell me that?   40
His son was but a ward two years ago.

Romeo. (to a Servingman) What lady's that, which
doth enrich the hand

          Of yonder knight?

Servingman. I know not, sir.

Romeo. O, she doth teach the torches to burn bright!   45
It seems she hangs upon the cheek of night
As a rich jewel in an Ethiop's ear —
Beauty too rich for use, for earth too dear!
So shows a snowy dove trooping with crows
As yonder lady o'er her fellows shows.   50
The measure done, I'll watch her place to stand
And, touching hers, make blessèd my rude hand.
Did my heart love till now? Forswear it, sight!
For I ne'er saw true beauty till this night.

---

30 *unlooked-for sport* a dance was not originally planned 34 *thirty
years* indicating Capulet's advanced age 41 *His son . . . ago* it
seems only two years since his son was a minor 52 *rude* coarse-
skinned

55   *Tybalt.* This, by his voice, should be a Montague.
        Fetch me my rapier, boy. What, dares the slave
        Come hither, covered with an antic face,
        To fleer and scorn at our solemnity?
        Now, by the stock and honor of my kin,
60   To strike him dead I hold it not a sin.
    Capulet. Why, how now, kinsman? Wherefore storm
        you so?
    Tybalt. Uncle, this is a Montague, our foe;
        A villain, that is hither come in spite
        To scorn at our solemnity this night.
    Capulet. Young Romeo is it?
65   *Tybalt.*   'Tis he, that villain Romeo.
    Capulet. Content thee, gentle coz, let him alone.
        'A bears him like a portly gentleman,
        And, to say truth, Verona brags of him
        To be a virtuous and well-governed youth.
70   I would not for the wealth of all this town
        Here in my house do him disparagement.
        Therefore be patient, take no note of him.
        It is my will, the which if thou respect,
        Show a fair presence and put off these frowns.
75   An ill-beseeming semblance for a feast.
    Tybalt. It fits when such a villain is a guest.
        I'll not endure him.
    Capulet.   He shall be endured.
        What, goodman boy! I say he shall. Go to!
        Am I the master here, or you? Go to!
80   You'll endure him, God shall mend my soul!
        You'll make a mutiny among my guests!
        You will set cock-a-hoop, you'll be the man!
    Tybalt. Why, uncle, 'tis a shame.

---

57 *antic face* comic mask 58 *fleer* mock *solemnity* dignified feast
67 *portly* of good carriage 80 *God . . . soul* an expression of im-
patience 81 *mutiny* violent disturbance 82 *set cock-a-hoop* i.e.
take the lead *be the man* play the big man

Capulet.   Go to, go to!
 You are a saucy boy. Is't so, indeed?
 This trick may chance to scathe you. I know what. 85
 You must contrary me! Marry, 'tis time —
 Well said, my hearts! — You are a princox — go!
 Be quiet, or — More light, more light! — For
  shame!
 I'll make you quiet; what! — Cheerly, my hearts!
Tybalt. Patience perforce with willful choler meeting 90
 Makes my flesh tremble in their different greeting.
 I will withdraw; but this intrusion shall,
 Now seeming sweet, convert to bitt'rest gall. *Exit.*
Romeo. If I profane with my unworthiest hand
  This holy shrine, the gentle sin is this; 95
 My lips, two blushing pilgrims, ready stand
  To smooth that rough touch with a tender kiss.
Juliet. Good pilgrim, you do wrong your hand too
  much,
  Which mannerly devotion shows in this;
 For saints have hands that pilgrims' hands do touch, 100
  And palm to palm is holy palmers' kiss.
Romeo. Have not saints lips, and holy palmers too?
Juliet. Ay, pilgrim, lips that they must use in prayer.
Romeo. O, then, dear saint, let lips do what hands do!
  They pray; grant thou, lest faith turn to despair. 105
Juliet. Saints do not move, though grant for prayers'
  sake.
Romeo. Then move not while my prayer's effect I take.
 Thus from my lips, by thine my sin is purged.
  (*Kisses her.*)

---

85 *scathe* injure *what* what I'm doing 86 *'tis time* it's time you
learned your place 87 *said* done *my hearts* addressed to the
dancers *princox* saucy boy 90 *Patience perforce* enforced self-
restraint *choler* anger 94–111 these lines form an English-style
sonnet and the first quatrain of another 95 *shrine* i.e. Juliet's
hand *sin* i.e. roughening her soft hand with his coarse one 96
pilgrims so called because pilgrims visit shrines 98–101 *Good . . .
kiss* your touch is not rough, to heal it with a kiss is unnecessary, a
handclasp is sufficient greeting 101 *palmers* religious pilgrims 104
do what hands do i.e. press each other (in a kiss) 106 *move* take
the initiative *grant* give permission

Juliet. Then have my lips the sin that they have took.

110 *Romeo.* Sin from my lips? O trespass sweetly urged!
    Give me my sin again.   (*Kisses her.*)
Juliet.   You kiss by th' book.
Nurse. Madam, your mother craves a word with you.
Romeo. What is her mother?
Nurse.   Marry, bachelor,
    Her mother is the lady of the house,
115 And a good lady, and a wise and virtuous.
    I nursed her daughter that you talked withal.
    I tell you, he that can lay hold of her
    Shall have the chinks.
Romeo.   Is she a Capulet?
    O dear account! my life is my foe's debt.
120 *Benvolio.* Away, be gone; the sport is at the best.
Romeo. Ay, so I fear; the more is my unrest.
Capulet. Nay, gentlemen, prepare not to be gone;
    We have a trifling foolish banquet towards.
    Is it e'en so? Why then, I thank you all.
125 I thank you, honest gentlemen. Good night.
    More torches here! Come on then, let's to bed.
    Ah, sirrah, by my fay, it waxes late;
    I'll to my rest.   *Exit all but Juliet and Nurse.*
Juliet. Come hither, nurse. What is yond gentleman?
130 *Nurse.* The son and heir of old Tiberio.
Juliet. What's he that now is going out of door?
Nurse. Marry, that, I think, be young Petruchio.
Juliet. What's he that follows there, that would not
    dance?
Nurse. I know not.
135 *Juliet.* Go ask his name — If he be marrièd,
    My grave is like to be my wedding bed.

---

111 *book* book of etiquette 116 *withal* with 118 *chinks* money 119
my foe's debt owed to my foe 123 *banquet* light refreshments *to-*
wards in preparation 127 *fay* faith

Nurse. His name is Romeo, and a Montague,
  The only son of your great enemy.
Juliet. My only love, sprung from my only hate!
  Too early seen unknown, and known too late! 140
  Prodigious birth of love it is to me
  That I must love a loathèd enemy.
Nurse. What's this? what's this?
Juliet.   A rhyme I learnt even now
  Of one I danced withal. *One calls within,* "Juliet."
Nurse.   Anon, anon!
  Come, let's away; the strangers all are gone. *Exit.* 145

141 *Prodigious* monstrous 144 *Anon* i.e. we are coming right away

ACT II

Enter Chorus.

Chorus. Now old desire doth in his deathbed lie,
 And young affection gapes to be his heir;
That fair for which love groaned for and would die,
 With tender Juliet matched, is now not fair.
Now Romeo is beloved and loves again,
5 Alike bewitchèd by the charm of looks;
But to his foe supposed he must complain,
 And she steal love's sweet bait from fearful hooks.
Being held a foe, he may not have access
 To breathe such vows as lovers use to swear,
10 And she as much in love, her means much less
 To meet her new belovèd anywhere;
But passion lends them power, time means, to meet
Temp'ring extremities with extreme sweet. *Exit.*

ACT II, SCENE I

Enter Romeo alone.

Romeo. Can I go forward when my heart is here?
 Turn back, dull earth, and find thy centre out.

II, Cho., 1 *old desire* i.e. Romeo's love of Rosaline 2 *young affection* new love *gapes* opens his mouth hungrily 7 *complain* make a lover's plaints 8 *steal . . . hooks* a popular conceit: the lover "fishes" for his beloved. For Juliet to be "caught" is dangerous because of the family feud 10 *use* are accustomed II, i, 1 *my heart is here* the Neo-Platonic fancy that the heart or soul of the lover dwells in the beloved 2 *earth* i.e. my body *centre,* i.e. my heart or soul

Enter Benvolio with Mercutio. Romeo retires.

Benvolio. Romeo! my cousin Romeo! Romeo!
Mercutio.   He is wise,
  And, on my life, hath stol'n him home to bed.
Benvolio. He ran this way and leapt this orchard wall.   5
  Call, good Mercutio.
Mercutio.   Nay, I'll conjure too.
  Romeo! humors! madman! passion! lover!
  Appear thou in the likeness of a sigh;
  Speak but one rhyme, and I am satisfied!
  Cry but "Ay me!" pronounce but "love" and
    "dove";   10
  Speak to my gossip Venus one fair word,
  One nickname for her purblind son and heir
  Young Abraham Cupid, he that shot so true
  When King Cophetua loved the beggar maid!
  He heareth not, he stirreth not, he moveth not;   15
  The ape is dead, and I must conjure him.
  I conjure thee by Rosaline's bright eyes,
  By her high forehead and her scarlet lip,
  By her fine foot, straight leg, and quivering thigh,
  And the demesnes that there adjacent lie,   20
  That in thy likeness thou appear to us!
Benvolio. An if he hear thee, thou wilt anger him.
Mercutio. This cannot anger him. 'Twould anger him
  To raise a spirit in his mistress' circle
  Of some strange nature, letting it there stand   25
  Till she had laid it and conjured it down.
  That were some spite; my invocation
  Is fair and honest: in his mistress' name,
  I conjure only but to raise up him.

---

7 *humors* whims   11 *gossip* female crony   12 *purblind* dim-sighted
13 *Young Abraham* youthful, yet patriarchal (Cupid, or Love, was
both the youngest and the oldest of the gods)   14 *King Cophetua .
. . . beggar maid* from a popular ballad   16 *The ape . . . him* prob-
ably recalling a showman's ape who "played dead" until called
with the right word-formula   20 *demesnes* domains   24 *circle* the
conjurer's circle in which an evoked spirit supposedly appears

Benvolio. Come, he hath hid himself among these
30   trees
        To be consorted with the humorous night.
        Blind is his love and best befits the dark.
Mercutio. If love be blind, love cannot hit the mark.
        Now will he sit under a medlar tree
35   And wish his mistress were that kind of fruit
        As maids call medlars when they laugh alone.
        O, Romeo, that she were, O that she were
        An open et cetera, thou a pop'rin pear!
        Romeo, good night. I'll to my truckle-bed;
40   This field-bed is too cold for me to sleep.
        Come, shall we go?
Benvolio.   Go then, for 'tis in vain
        To seek him here that means not to be found.
                                        Exit (with others).

ACT II, SCENE II

Romeo. (*coming forward*) He jests at scars that never
        felt a wound.

        Enter Juliet above at a window.

        But soft; What light through yonder window breaks?
        It is the East, and Juliet is the sun!
        Arise, fair sun, and kill the envious moon,
5   Who is already sick and pale with grief
        That thou her maid art far more fair than she.

---

31 *humorous* damp: also, capricious 36, 38 *medlars, pop'rin pear*
fruits 39 *truckle-bed* trundle-bed II, ii, 4 *kill* make invisible by
more intense light 6 *her maid* Diana, moon-goddess, was patroness
of virgins

Be not her maid, since she is envious.
Her vestal livery is but sick and green,
And none but fools do wear it. Cast it off.
It is my lady; O, it is my love!   10
O that she knew she were!
She speaks, yet she says nothing. What of that?
Her eye discourses; I will answer it.
I am too bold; 'tis not to me she speaks.
Two of the fairest stars in all the heaven,   15
Having some business, do entreat her eyes
To twinkle in their spheres till they return.
What if her eyes were there, they in her head?
The brightness of her cheek would shame those stars
As daylight doth a lamp; her eyes in heaven   20
Would through the airy region stream so bright
That birds would sing and think it were not night.
See how she leans her cheek upon her hand!
O that I were a glove upon that hand,
That I might touch that cheek!

Juliet.   Ay me!
Romeo.   She speaks.   25
O, speak again, bright angel! for thou art
As glorious to this night, being o'er my head,
As is a wingèd messenger of heaven
Unto the white-upturnèd wond'ring eyes
Of mortals that fall back to gaze on him   30
When he bestrides the lazy-pacing clouds
And sails upon the bosom of the air.

Juliet. O Romeo, Romeo! wherefore art thou Romeo?
Deny thy father and refuse thy name;
Or, if thou wilt not, be but sworn my love,   35
And I'll no longer be a Capulet.

---

8 *vestal livery* virginity (after Vesta, another virgin goddess) *green*
anaemic   17 *spheres* orbits   29 *white-upturnèd* the whites show when
the eyes are turned upward

Romeo. (*aside*) Shall I hear more, or shall I speak at
    this?
Juliet. 'Tis but thy name that is my enemy.
    Thou art thyself, though not a Montague.
40   What's Montague? It is nor hand, nor foot,
    Nor arm, nor face, nor any other part
    Belonging to a man. O, be some other name!
    What's in a name? That which we call a rose
    By any other name would smell as sweet.
45   So Romeo would, were he not Romeo called,
    Retain that dear perfection which he owes
    Without that title. Romeo, doff thy name;
    And for thy name, which is no part of thee,
    Take all myself.
Romeo.   I take thee at thy word.
50   Call me but love, and I'll be new baptized;
    Henceforth I never will be Romeo.
Juliet. What man art thou that, thus bescreened in
    night,
    So stumblest on my counsel?
Romeo.   By a name
    I know not how to tell thee who I am.
55   My name, dear saint, is hateful to myself,
    Because it is an enemy to thee.
    Had I it written, I would tear the word.
Juliet. My ears have yet not drunk a hundred words
    Of thy tongue's uttering, yet I know the sound.
60   Art thou not Romeo, and a Montague?
Romeo. Neither, fair maid, if either thee dislike.
Juliet. How camest thou hither, tell me, and wherefore?
    The orchard walls are high and hard to climb,
    And the place death, considering who thou art,
65   If any of my kinsmen find thee here.
Romeo. With love's light wings did I o'erperch these
    walls;

---

46 *owes* owns   61 *dislike* displease   66 *o'erperch* fly over

    For stony limits cannot hold love out,
    And what love can do, that dares love attempt.
    Therefore thy kinsmen are no stop to me.
Juliet. If they do see thee, they will murder thee.   70
Romeo. Alack, there lies more peril in thine eye
    Than twenty of their swords! Look thou but sweet,
    And I am proof against their enmity.
Juliet. I would not for the world they saw thee here.
Romeo. I have night's cloak to hide me from their
      eyes;   75
    And but thou love me, let them find me here.
    My life were better ended by their hate
    Than death proroguèd, wanting of thy love.
Juliet. By whose direction found'st thou out this place?
Romeo. By love, that first did prompt me to inquire.   80
    He lent me counsel, and I lent him eyes.
    I am no pilot; yet, wert thou as far
    As that vast shore washed with the farthest sea,
    I should adventure for such merchandise.
Juliet. Thou knowest the mask of night is on my face;   85
    Else would a maiden blush bepaint my cheek
    For that which thou hast heard me speak tonight.
    Fain would I dwell on form — fain, fain deny
    What I have spoke; but farewell compliment!
    Dost thou love me? I know thou wilt say "Ay";   90
    And I will take thy word. Yet, if thou swear'st,
    Thou mayst prove false. At lovers' perjuries,
    They say Jove laughs. O gentle Romeo,
    If thou dost love, pronounce it faithfully.
    Or if thou thinkest I am too quickly won,   95
    I'll frown, and be perverse, and say thee nay,
    So thou wilt woo; but else, not for the world.
    In truth, fair Montague, I am too fond,
    And therefore thou mayst think my havior light;

---

73 *proof* armored 78 *proroguèd* postponed *wanting of* lacking
83 *farthest sea* the Pacific 84 *adventure* risk a voyage 89 *com-
pliment* etiquette 99 *havior* behavior

100 But trust me, gentleman, I'll prove more true
Than those that have more cunning to be strange.
I should have been more strange, I must confess,
But that thou overheard'st, ere I was ware,
My true-love passion. Therefore pardon me,
105 And not impute this yielding to light love,
Which the dark night hath so discoverèd.
Romeo. Lady, by yonder blessèd moon I vow,
That tips with silver all these fruit-tree tops —
Juliet. O, swear not by the moon, th' inconstant moon,
110 That monthly changes in her circled orb,
Lest that thy love prove likewise variable.
Romeo. What shall I swear by?
Juliet.   Do not swear at all;
Or if thou wilt, swear by thy gracious self,
Which is the god of my idolatry,
And I'll believe thee.
115 *Romeo.*   If my heart's dear love —
Juliet. Well, do not swear. Although I joy in thee,
I have no joy of this contract tonight.
It is too rash, too unadvised, too sudden;
Too like the lightning, which doth cease to be
120 Ere one can say; "It lightens." Sweet, good night!
This bud of love, by summer's ripening breath,
May prove a beauteous flow'r when next we meet.
Good night, good night! As sweet repose and rest
Come to thy heart as that within my breast!
125 *Romeo.* O, wilt thou leave me so unsatisfied?
Juliet. What satisfaction canst thou have tonight?
Romeo. Th' exchange of thy love's faithful vow for
mine.
Juliet. I gave thee mine before thou didst request it;
And yet I would it were to give again.
Romeo. Wouldst thou withdraw it? For what purpose,
130   love?

---

101 *strange* aloof, distant   103 *ware* aware of you   106 *discoverèd*
revealed

Juliet. But to be frank and give it thee again.
   And yet I wish but for the thing I have.
   My bounty is as boundless as the sea,
   My love as deep; the more I give to thee,
   The more I have, for both are infinite.   135
   I hear some noise within. Dear love, adieu!
                     (*Nurse calls within.*)
   Anon, good nurse! Sweet Montague, be true.
   Stay but a little, I will come again.   *Exit.*
Romeo. O blessèd, blessèd night! I am afeard,
   Being in night, all this is but a dream,   140
   Too flattering-sweet to be substantial.

Enter Juliet above.

Juliet. Three words, dear Romeo, and good night
    indeed.
   If that thy bent of love be honorable,
   Thy purpose marriage, send me word tomorrow,
   By one that I'll procure to come to thee,   145
   Where and what time thou wilt perform the rite;
   And all my fortunes at thy foot I'll lay
   And follow thee my lord throughout the world.
Nurse. (*within*) Madam!
Juliet. I come, anon. — But if thou meanest not well,   150
   I do beseech thee —
Nurse. (*within*) Madam!
Juliet.   By and by I come. —
   To cease thy suit and leave me to my grief.
   Tomorrow will I send.
Romeo.   So thrive my soul —
Juliet. A thousand times good night!   *Exit.*   155

---

131 *frank* generous 133 *bounty* wish to give (love) 135 *The more
I have* scholastic theologians debated how love could be given
away and yet the giver have more than before 143 *bent* purpose
152 *By and by* immediately

Romeo. A thousand times the worse, to want thy light!
    Love goes toward love as schoolboys from their
      books;
    But love from love, toward school with heavy looks.

Enter Juliet (above) again.

Juliet. Hist! Romeo, hist! O for a falc'ner's voice
160   To lure this tassel-gentle back again!
    Bondage is hoarse and may not speak aloud,
    Else would I tear the cave where Echo lies
    And make her airy tongue more hoarse than mine
    With repetition of "My Romeo!"
165 *Romeo.* It is my soul that calls upon my name.
    How silver-sweet sound lovers' tongues by night,
    Like softest music to attending ears!
Juliet. Romeo!
Romeo.   My sweet?
Juliet.   At what o'clock tomorrow
    Shall I send to thee?
Romeo.   By the hour of nine.
170 *Juliet.* I will not fail. 'Tis twenty years till then.
    I have forgot why I did call thee back.
Romeo. Let me stand here till thou remember it.
Juliet. I shall forget, to have thee still stand there,
    Rememb'ring how I love thy company.
175 *Romeo.* And I'll still stay, to have thee still forget,
    Forgetting any other home but this.
Juliet. 'Tis almost morning. I would have thee gone —
    And yet no farther than a wanton's bird,
    That lets it hop a little from her hand,
180   Like a poor prisoner in his twisted gyves,
    And with a silken thread plucks it back again,
    So loving-jealous of his liberty.

---

160 *tassel-gentle* tiercel-gentle, or male falcon 161 *Bondage* she
feels "imprisoned" by the nearness of her kinsmen 167 *attending*
paying attention 178 *wanton* spoiled child 180 *gyves* fetters

Romeo. I would I were thy bird.
Juliet.   Sweet, so would I.
   Yet I should kill thee with much cherishing.
   Good night, good night! Parting is such sweet
      sorrow   185
   That I shall say good night till it be morrow.   *Exit.*
Romeo. Sleep dwell upon thine eyes, peace in thy
      breast!
   Would I were sleep and peace, so sweet to rest!
   Hence will I to my ghostly father's cell,
   His help to crave and my dear hap to tell.   *Exit.*   190

ACT II, SCENE III

Enter Friar Laurence alone, with a basket.

Friar. The grey-eyed morn smiles on the frowning
      night,
   Check'ring the Eastern clouds with streaks of light;
   And fleckèd darkness like a drunkard reels
   From forth day's path and Titan's fiery wheels.
   Now, ere the sun advance his burning eye   5
   The day to cheer and night's dank dew to dry,
   I must up-fill this osier cage of ours
   With baleful weeds and precious-juicèd flowers.
   The earth that's nature's mother is her tomb.

184 *cherishing* caressing 186 *morrow* morning 189 *ghostly* spiritual
190 *dear hap* good luck II, iii, 3 *fleckèd* spotted, dappled 4
Titan's fiery wheels the sun's chariot wheels 7 *osier cage* willow
basket

10   What is her burying grave, that is her womb;
And from her womb children of divers kind
We sucking on her natural bosom find,
Many for many virtues excellent,
None but for some, and yet all different.
15   O, mickle is the powerful grace that lies
In plants, herbs, stones, and their true qualities;
For naught so vile that on the earth doth live
But to the earth some special good doth give;
Nor aught so good but, strained from that fair use,
20   Revolts from true birth, stumbling on abuse.
Virtue itself turns vice, being misapplied,
And vice sometime's by action dignified.

Enter Ròmeo.

Within the infant rind of this weak flower
Poison hath residence, and medicine power;
For this, being smelt, with that part cheers each
25   part;
Being tasted, slays all senses with the heart.
Two such opposèd kings encamp them still
In man as well as herbs — grace and rude will;
And where the worser is predominant,
30   Full soon the canker death eats up that plant.
Romeo. Good morrow, father.
Friar.   Benedicite!
What early tongue so sweet saluteth me?
Young son, it argues a distemperèd head
So soon to bid good morrow to thy bed.
35   Care keeps his watch in every old man's eye,
And where care lodges, sleep will never lie;
But where unbruisèd youth with unstuffed brain
Doth couch his limbs, there golden sleep doth reign.

---

15 *mickle* much 20 *true birth* its true nature 22 *dignified* made
worthy 26 *being . . . heart* i.e. being smelt, stimulates; being tasted,
kills 27 *still* always 28 *grace* power of goodness *rude will* coarse
impulses of the flesh 30 *canker* the worm in the bud 31 *morrow*
morning *Benedicite* bless you 37 *unstuffed* carefree

Therefore thy earliness doth me assure
Thou art uproused with some distemp'rature;   40
Or if not so, then here I hit it right —
Our Romeo hath not been in bed tonight.

Romeo. That last is true — the sweeter rest was mine.

Friar. God pardon sin! Wast thou with Rosaline?

Romeo. With Rosaline, my ghostly father? No.   45
I have forgot that name and that name's woe.

Friar. That's my good son! But where hast thou been
then?

Romeo. I'll tell thee ere thou ask it me again.
I have been feasting with mine enemy,
Where on a sudden one hath wounded me   50
That's by me wounded. Both our remedies
Within thy help and holy physic lies.
I bear no hatred, blessèd man, for, lo,
My intercession likewise steads my foe.

Friar. Be plain, good son, and homely in thy drift. 55
Riddling confession finds but riddling shrift.

Romeo. Then plainly know my heart's dear love is set
On the fair daughter of rich Capulet;
As mine on hers, so hers is set on mine,
And all combined, save what thou must combine   60
By holy marriage. When, and where, and how
We met, we wooed, and made exchange of vow,
I'll tell thee as we pass; but this I pray,
That thou consent to marry us today.

Friar. Holy Saint Francis! What a change is here!   65
Is Rosaline, that thou didst love so dear,
So soon forsaken? Young men's love then lies
Not truly in their hearts, but in their eyes.
Jesu Maria! What a deal of brine
Hath washed thy sallow cheeks for Rosaline!   70
How much salt water thrown away in waste
To season love, that of it doth not taste!

---

52 *physic* medicine 54 *intercession* request *steads* benefits 55
homely simple *drift* explanation 56 *shrift* absolution 72 *season*
flavor *doth not taste* i.e. now has no savor

The sun not yet thy sighs from heaven clears,
Thy old groans ring yet in mine ancient ears.
75 Lo, here upon thy cheek the stain doth sit
Of an old tear that is not washed off yet.
If e'er thou wast thyself, and these woes thine,
Thou and these woes were all for Rosaline.
And art thou changed? Pronounce this sentence
then:
80 Women may fall when there's no strength in men.
Romeo. Thou chid'st me oft for loving Rosaline.
Friar. For doting, not for loving, pupil mine.
Romeo. And bad'st me bury love.
Friar.   Not in a grave
To lay one in, another out to have.
85 *Romeo.* I pray thee chide not. She whom I love now
Doth grace for grace and love for love allow.
The other did not so.
Friar.   O, she knew well
Thy love did read by rote, that could not spell.
But come, young waverer, come go with me.
90 In one respect I'll thy assistant be;
For this alliance may so happy prove
To turn your households' rancor to pure love.
Romeo. O, let us hence! I stand on sudden haste.
Friar. Wisely and slow. They stumble that run fast.
Exit.

80 *strength* constancy   86 *grace* favor   88 *by rote . . . spell* like a
child repeating words without understanding them   93 *on* in need of

ACT II, SCENE IV

Enter Benvolio and Mercutio.

Mercutio. Where the devil should this Romeo be?
   Came he not home tonight?

Benvolio. Not to his father's. I spoke with his man.

Mercutio. Why, that same pale hard-hearted wench,
      that Rosaline,
   Torments him so that he will sure run mad.   5

Benvolio. Tybalt, the kinsman to old Capulet,
   Hath sent a letter to his father's house.

Mercutio. A challenge, on my life.

Benvolio. Romeo will answer it.

Mercutio. Any man that can write may answer a letter.   10

Benvolio. Nay, he will answer the letter's master, how
   he dares, being dared.

Mercutio. Alas, poor Romeo, he is already dead! stabbed
   with a white wench's black eye; run through the ear
   with a love song; the very pin of his heart cleft   15
   with the blind bow-boy's butt-shaft; and is he a man
   to encounter Tybalt?

Benvolio. Why, what is Tybalt?

Mercutio. More than Prince of Cats, I can tell you. O,
   he's the courageous captain of compliments. He   20
   fights as you sing pricksong — keeps time, distance,
   and proportion; he rests his minim rests, one, two,
   and the third in your bosom! the very butcher of a

II, iv, 15 *pin* peg in the centre of a target, bull's-eye 16 *bow-boy's butt-shaft* Cupid's arrow (jestingly identified as a barbless target-arrow) 16–17 *is . . . Tybalt* Mercutio has doubts of Romeo's prowess while he is despondent and low-spirited 19 *Prince of Cats* Tybalt, or Tybert, is the cat's name in mediaeval stories of Reynard the Fox 20 *compliments* etiquette 21 *pricksong* written music 22 *minim rests* shortest rests (in the old musical notation) 23 *third* third rapier thrust

silk button, a duellist, a duellist! a gentleman of the
25   very first house, of the first and second cause. Ah,
the immortal passado! the punto reverso! the hay!
Benvolio. The what?
Mercutio. The pox of such antic, lisping, affecting
fantasticoes — these new tuners of accent! "By Jesu,
30   a very good blade! a very tall man! a very good
whore!" Why, is not this a lamentable thing, grandsir, that we should be thus afflicted with these strange
flies, these fashion-mongers, these pardon-me's, who
stand so much on the new form that they cannot sit
35   at ease on the old bench? O, their bones, their
bones!

Enter Romeo.

Benvolio. Here comes Romeo! here comes Romeo!
Mercutio. Without his roe, like a dried herring. O flesh,
flesh, how art thou fishified! Now is he for the num-
40   bers that Petrarch flowed in. Laura, to his lady, was
a kitchen wench (marry, she had a better love to
berhyme her), Dido a dowdy, Cleopatra a gypsy,
Helen and Hero hildings and harlots, This be a grey
eye or so, but not to the purpose. Signior Romeo,
45   bonjour! There's a French salutation to your French
slop. You gave us the counterfeit fairly last night.
Romeo. Good morrow to you both. What counterfeit
did I give you?
Mercutio. The slip, sir, the slip. Can you not conceive?

24 *button* i.e. on his opponent's shirt   25 *first house* finest fencing
school   *first and second cause* causes for a challenge (in the
duellist's code)   26 *passado* lunge   *punto reverso* backhanded stroke
hay ~ome-thrust (from *hai*, 'I have it"; a new term to Benvolio)
29 *fantasticoes* coxcombs   30 *tall* brave   31–32 *grandsir* good sir   33
pardon-me's i.e. sticklers for etiquette   34 *form* (1) fashion (2) school-
bench   35 *old bench* i.e. native manners and learning   *bones* "bon's"
(Fr. "good's")   38 *Without his roe* i.e. "shot"   39–40 *numbers*
verses   40 *Petrarch* famed fourteenth-century Italian poet, author of
Lives, a series of biographies of famous people   *Laura* Petrarch's
beloved *to* in comparison with   42 *Dido* Queen of Carthage who fell
in love with Aeneas   43 *Helen* Helen of Troy   *Hero* beloved of
Leander   *hildings* worthless creatures   *Thisbe* Pyramus and Thisbe
were young lovers whose story resembles that of Romeo and Juliet
44 *not to the purpose* not worth mentioning   45 *bonjour* good
day   46 *slop* trousers   *fairly* effectively   49 *slip* (1) escape (2)
counterfeit coin

Romeo. Pardon, good Mercutio. My business was great,   50
and in such a case as mine a man may strain
courtesy.

Mercutio. That's as much as to say, such a case as
yours constrains a man to bow in the hams.

Romeo. Meaning, to curtsy.   55

Mercutio. Thou hast most kindly hit it.

Romeo. A most courteous exposition.

Mercutio. Nay, I am the very pink of courtesy.

Romeo. Pink for flower.

Mercutio. Right.   60

Romeo. Why, then is my pump well-flowered.

Mercutio. Sure wit, follow me this jest now till thou
hast worn out thy pump, that, when the single sole
of it is worn, the jest may remain, after the wearing,
solely singular.   65

Romeo. O single-soled jest, solely singular for the singleness!

Mercutio. Come between us, good Benvolio! My wits
faint.

Romeo. Swits and spurs, swits and spurs! or I'll cry a   70
match.

Mercutio. Nay, if our wits run the wild-goose chase, I
am done; for thou hast more of the wild goose in
one of thy wits than, I am sure, I have in my whole
five. Was I with you there for the goose?   75

Romeo. Thou wast never with me for anything when
thou wast not there for the goose.

Mercutio. I will bite thee by the ear for that jest.

Romeo. Nay, good goose, bite not!

53-54 *such . . . yours* the pox (implied)   54 *hams* hips   56 *kindly
hit it* interpreted it in your own way   59 *flower* "flower of courtesy"
was the usual complimentary form   61 *pump* shoe   *well-flowered*
because pinked, or punched, with an ornamental design   65
solely singular uniquely remarkable   66 *single-soled* weak   66-67
singleness weakness   68-69 *My wits faint* my mind fails in this in-
tricate word play   70 *Swits and spurs* switches and spurs, i.e. keep
your horse (wit) running   *cry a match* claim victory   72 *wild-goose
chase* cross-country horse race of "follow the leader"   75 *Was . . .
goose?* was I accurate in calling you a goose?   76-77 *Thou . . .
goose* you were never in my company for any purpose when you
weren't looking for a prostitute (goose)   79 *good . . . not* spare
me (proverbial)

80 *Mercutio.* Thy wit is a very bitter sweeting; it is a most
    sharp sauce.

Romeo. And is it not, then, well served in to a sweet
    goose?

Mercutio. O, here's a wit of cheveril, that stretches
85   from an inch narrow to an ell broad!

Romeo. I stretch it out for that word "broad," which,
    added to the goose, proves thee far and wide a broad
    goose.

Mercutio. Why, is not this better now than groaning
90   for love? Now art thou sociable, now art thou
    Romeo; now art thou what thou art, by art as well
    as by nature. For this drivelling love is like a great
    natural that runs lolling up and down to hide his
    bauble in a hole.

95 *Benvolio.* Stop there, stop there!

Mercutio. Thou desirest me to stop in my tale against
    the hair.

Benvolio. Thou wouldst else have made thy tale large.

Mercutio. O, thou art deceived! I would have made it
100   short; for I was come to the whole depth of my tale,
    and meant indeed to occupy the argument no longer.

Romeo. Here's goodly gear!

Enter Nurse and her man Peter.

Mercutio. A sail, a sail!

Benvolio. Two, two! a shirt and a smock.

105 *Nurse.* Peter!

Peter. Anon.

Nurse. My fan, Peter.

---

80 *bitter sweeting* a tart species of apple   82 *sweet* tasty, tender   84
cheveril, kid-skin, easily stretched   85 *ell* 45 inches (English measure)
87–88 *broad goose* possibly, a goose from the Broads, shallow Norfolk
lakes   93 *natural* idiot   94 *bauble* jester's wand   96–97 *against the
hair* with my hair rubbed the wrong way, against my inclination   98
large broad, indecent   101 *occupy the argument* pursue the subject
102 *gear* stuff   104 *shirt, smock* male and female garments

Mercutio. Good Peter, to hide her face; for her fan's the fairer face.

Nurse. God ye good morrow, gentlemen. 110

Mercutio. God ye good-den, fair gentlewoman.

Nurse. Is it good-den?

Mercutio. 'Tis no less, I tell ye; for the bawdy hand of the dial is now upon the prick of noon.

Nurse. Out upon you! What a man are you! 115

Romeo. One, gentlewoman, that God hath made for himself to mar.

Nurse. By my troth, it is well said. "For himself to mar," quoth 'a? Gentlemen, can any of you tell me where I may find the young Romeo? 120

Romeo. I can tell you; but young Romeo will be older when you have found him than he was when you sought him. I am the youngest of that name, for fault of a worse.

Nurse. You say well. 125

Mercutio. Yea, is the worst well? Very well took, i' faith! wisely, wisely.

Nurse. If you be he, sir, I desire some confidence with you.

Benvolio. She will endite him to some supper. 130

Mercutio. A bawd, a bawd, a bawd! So ho!

Romeo. What hast thou found?

Mercutio. No hare, sir; unless a hare, sir, in a lenten pie, that is something stale and hoar ere it be spent.

He walks by them and sings.

112 *Is it good-den?* is it already afternoon? 114 *prick* indented point on a clock-face or sundial 119 *quoth 'a* said he 123-124 *for . . . worse* parodying "for want of a better" 126 *took* understood 128 *confidence* conference (malapropism: the humorous misuse of a word which sounds somewhat like the intended word, but is totally wrong in the context used) 130 *endite* invite (anticipating a malapropism) 131 *So ho* hunter's cry on sighting game 133 *hare* i.e. prostitute *lenten pie* meat pie eaten sparingly during Lent 134 *hoar* (1) grey with mould (2) grey-haired

135   An old hare hoar,
                     And an old hare hoar,
                     Is very good meat in Lent;
                     But a hare that is hoar
                     Is too much for a score
140   When it hoars ere it be spent.

     Romeo, will you come to your father's? We'll to
        dinner thither.
     Romeo. I will follow you.
     Mercutio. Farewell, ancient lady. Farewell,
145   (*sings*) lady, lady, lady.   *Exit Mercutio, Benvolio.*
     Nurse. I pray you, sir, what saucy merchant was this
        that was so full of his ropery?
     Romeo. A gentleman, nurse, that loves to hear himself
        talk and will speak more in a minute than he will
150   stand to in a month.
     Nurse. An 'a speak anything against me, I'll take him
        down, an 'a were lustier than he is, and twenty such
        Jacks; and if I cannot, I'll find those that shall.
        Scurvy knave! I am none of his flirt-gills; I am none
155   of his skains-mates. And thou must stand by too,
        and suffer every knave to use me at his pleasure!
     Peter. I saw no man use you at his pleasure. If I had,
        my weapon should quickly have been out, I warrant
        you. I dare draw as soon as another man, if I see
160   occasion in a good quarrel, and the law on my side.
     Nurse. Now, afore God, I am so vexed that every part
        about me quivers. Scurvy knave! Pray you, sir, a
        word; and, as I told you, my young lady bid me in-
        quire you out. What she bid me say, I will keep to
165   myself; but first let me tell ye, if ye should lead her
        into a fool's paradise, as they say, it were a very gross
        kind of behavior, as they say; for the gentlewoman is

145 *lady, lady, lady* ballad refrain from *Chaste Susanna*   147 *ropery*
vulgar jesting   154 *flirt-gills* flirting Jills   155 *skains-mates* outlaws,
gangster molls   165–166 *lead . . . paradise* let her think you plan to
marry her when you don't (proverbial)

young; and therefore, if you should deal double with
her, truly it were an ill thing to be offered to any
gentlewoman, and very weak dealing.   170

Romeo. Nurse, commend me to thy lady and mistress.
I protest unto thee —

Nurse. Good heart, and i' faith I will tell her as much.
Lord, Lord! she will be a joyful woman.

Romeo. What wilt thou tell her, nurse? Thou dost not   175
mark me.

Nurse. I will tell her, sir, that you do protest, which, as
I take it, is a gentlemanlike offer.

Romeo. Bid her devise
Some means to come to shrift this afternoon;   180
And there she shall at Friar Laurence' cell
Be shrived and married. Here is for thy pains.

Nurse. No, truly, sir; not a penny.

Romeo. Go to! I say you shall.

Nurse. This afternoon, sir? Well, she shall be there.   185

Romeo. And stay, good nurse, behind the abbey wall.
Within this hour my man shall be with thee
And bring thee cords made like a tackled stair,
Which to the high topgallant of my joy
Must be my convoy in the secret night.   190
Farewell. Be trusty, and I'll quit thy pains.
Farewell. Commend me to thy mistress.

Nurse. Now God in heaven bless thee! Hark you, sir.

Romeo. What say'st thou, my dear nurse?

Nurse. Is your man secret? Did you ne'er hear say,   195
Two may keep counsel, putting one away?

Romeo. I warrant thee my man's as true as steel.

Nurse. Well, sir, my mistress is the sweetest lady. Lord,
Lord! when 'twas a little prating thing — O, there
is a nobleman in town, one Paris, that would fain   200
lay knife aboard; but she, good soul, had as lieve see

---

170 *weak* unmanly 188 *tackled stair* rope ladder 189 *topgallant*
mast and sail above the mainmast 190 *convoy* conveyance 191 *quit
thy pains* reward your efforts 201 *lay knife aboard* i.e. partake
of this dish *lieve* willingly

a toad, a very toad, as see him. I anger her sometimes, and tell her that Paris is the properer man;
but I'll warrant you, when I say so, she looks as pale
205   as any clout in the versal world. Doth not rosemary
and Romeo begin both with a letter?

Romeo. Ay, nurse; what of that? Both with an R.

Nurse. Ah, mocker! that's the dog's name. R is for the
— No; I know it begins with some other letter;
210   and she hath the prettiest sententious of it, of you
and rosemary, that it would do you good to hear it.

Romeo. Commend me to thy lady.

Nurse. Ay, a thousand times. (*Exit Romeo.*) Peter!

Peter. Anon.

215 *Nurse.* Peter, take my fan, and go before, and apace.
Exit (after Peter).

ACT II, SCENE V

Enter Juliet.

Juliet. The clock struck nine when I did send the nurse;
In half an hour she promised to return.
Perchance she cannot meet him. That's not so.
O, she is lame! Love's heralds should be thoughts,
5   Which ten times faster glide than the sun's beams
Driving back shadows over low'ring hills.
Therefore do nimble-pinioned doves draw Love,
And therefore hath the wind-swift Cupid wings.
Now is the sun upon the highmost hill

---

205 *clout* cloth   *versal* universal   208 *dog's name* R was called "the
dog's letter," since the sound *r-r-r-r* supposedly resembles a dog's
growl. The Nurse thinks it an ugly sound.   210 *sententious* sentences
II, v. 7 *nimble-pinioned* swift-winged   *doves* Venus' birds, who draw
her chariot   9 *upon . . . hill* at the zenith

Of this day's journey, and from nine till twelve   10
Is three long hours; yet she is not come.
Had she affections and warm youthful blood,
She would be as swift in motion as a ball;
My words would bandy her to my sweet love,
And his to me.   15
But old folks, many feign as they were dead —
Unwieldy, slow, heavy and pale as lead.

Enter Nurse and Peter.

O God, she comes; O honey nurse, what news?
Hast thou met with him? Send thy man away.
Nurse. Peter, stay at the gate.   *Exit Peter.*   20
Juliet. Now, good sweet nurse — O Lord, why lookest
    thou sad?
Though news be sad, yet tell them merrily;
If good, thou shamest the music of sweet news
By playing it to me with so sour a face.
Nurse. I am aweary, give me leave awhile.   25
Fie, how my bones ache! What a jaunce have I had!
Juliet. I would thou hadst my bones, and I thy news.
Nay, come, I pray thee speak. Good, good nurse,
    speak.
Nurse. Jesu, what haste! Can you not stay awhile?
Do you not see that I am out of breath?   30
Juliet. How art thou out of breath when thou hast
    breath
To say to me that thou art out of breath?
The excuse that thou dost make in this delay
Is longer than the tale thou dost excuse.
Is thy news good or bad? Answer to that.   35
Say either, and I'll stay the circumstance.
Let me be satisfied, is't good or bad?

14 *bandy* speed, as in tennis   16 *old . . . dead* many persons speak
figuratively of old folks as being dead   25 *give me leave* let me alone
26 *jaunce* jolting   29 *stay* wait   36 *stay the circumstance* wait for
details

Nurse. Well, you have made a simple choice; you know
    not how to choose a man. Romeo? No, not he.
40   Though his face be better than any man's, yet his
    leg excels all men's; and for a hand and a foot, and
    a body, though they be not to be talked on, yet they
    are past compare. He is not the flower of courtesy,
    but, I'll warrant him, as gentle as a lamb. Go thy
45   ways, wench; serve God. What, have you dined at
    home?

Juliet. No, no. But all this did I know before.
    What says he of our marriage? What of that?

Nurse. Lord, how my head aches! What a head have I!
50   It beats as it would fall in twenty pieces.
    My back a t' other side — ah, my back, my back!
    Beshrew your heart for sending me about
    To catch my death with jauncing up and down!

Juliet. I' faith, I am sorry that thou art not well.
55   Sweet, sweet, sweet nurse, tell me, what says my love?

Nurse. Your love says, like an honest gentleman, and
    a courteous, and a kind, and a handsome, and, I
    warrant, a virtuous — Where is your mother?

Juliet. Where is my mother? Why, she is within.
60   Where should she be? How oddly thou repliest!
    "Your love says, like an honest gentleman,
    'Where is your mother?' "

Nurse.   O God's Lady dear!
    Are you so hot? Marry come up, I trow.
    Is this the poultice for my aching bones?
65   Henceforward do your messages yourself.

Juliet. Here's such a coil! Come, what says Romeo?

Nurse. Have you got leave to go to shrift today?

Juliet. I have.

Nurse. Then hie you hence to Friar Laurence' cell;
70   There stays a husband to make you a wife.
    Now comes the wanton blood up in your cheeks:

---

38 *simple* foolish 50 *a* on 51 *Beshrew* shame on 63 *hot* angry
Marry come up by the Virgin Mary, take your come-uppance
(penalty) *trow* trust 66 *coil* fuss

They'll be in scarlet straight at any news.
Hie you to church; I must another way,
To fetch a ladder, by the which your love
Must climb a bird's nest soon when it is dark.   75
I am the drudge, and toil in your delight;
But you shall bear the burden soon at night.
Go; I'll to dinner; hie you to the cell.
Juliet. Hie to high fortune! Honest nurse, farewell.
                                                Exit.

ACT II, SCENE VI

Enter Friar Laurence and Romeo.

Friar. So smile the heavens upon this holy act
That after-hours with sorrow chide us not!
Romeo. Amen, amen! But come what sorrow can,
It cannot countervail the exchange of joy
That one short minute gives me in her sight.   5
Do thou but close our hands with holy words,
Then love-devouring death do what he dare —
It is enough I may but call her mine.
Friar. These violent delights have violent ends
And in their triumph die, like fire and powder,   10
Which, as they kiss, consume. The sweetest honey
Is loathsome in his own deliciousness
And in the taste confounds the appetite.
Therefore love moderately: long love doth so;
Too swift arrives as tardy as to slow.   15

---

72 *in scarlet* Juliet blushes easily *straight* straightway 75 *climb
. . . nest* i.e. climb to Juliet's room II, vi, 4 *countervail* outweigh

Enter Juliet.

Here comes the lady. O, so light a foot
Will ne'er wear out the everlasting flint.
A lover may bestride the gossamer
That idles in the wanton summer air,

20   And yet not fall; so light is vanity.
Juliet. Good even to my ghostly confessor.
Friar. Romeo shall thank thee, daughter, for us both.
Juliet. As much to him, else is his thanks too much.
Romeo. Ah, Juliet, if the measure of thy joy

25   Be heaped like mine, and that thy skill be more
To blazon it, then sweeten with thy breath
This neighbor air, and let rich music's tongue
Unfold the imagined happiness that both
Receive in either by this dear encounter.

30   *Juliet.* Conceit, more rich in matter than in words,
Brags of his substance, not of ornament.
They are but beggars than can count their worth;
But my true love is grown to such excess
I cannot sum up sum of half my wealth.

35   *Friar.* Come, come with me, and we will make short
       work;
For, by your leaves, you shall not stay alone
Till Holy Church incorporate two in one.   *Exit.*

---

12 *Is loathsome* i.e. if eaten to excess   15 *Too . . . slow* proverbial   17 *wear . . . flint* suggested by the proverb "In time small
water drops will wear away the stone"   18 *gossamer* spider's web
20 *vanity* transitory earthly love (cf. Ecclesiastes 9:9)   21 *ghostly*
spiritual   23 *As much* the same greeting   25 *that if thy . . . more*
you sing better than I   26 *blazon* set forth   30–31 *Conceit . . .
ornament* my understanding is fixed upon the reality of my great
love, not upon a vocal expression of it

ACT III, SCENE I

Enter Mercutio, Benvolio, and men.

Benvolio. I pray thee, good Mercutio, let's retire.
The day is hot, the Capulets abroad,
And, if we meet, we shall not 'scape a brawl,
For now, these hot days, is the mad blood stirring.

Mercutio. Thou art like one of these fellows that, when 5
he enters the confines of a tavern, claps me his sword
upon the table and says "God send me no need of
thee!" and by the operation of the second cup draws
him on the drawer, when indeed there is no need.

Benvolio. Am I like such a fellow? 10

Mercutio. Come, come, thou art as hot a jack in thy
mood as any in Italy; and as soon moved to be
moody, and as soon moody to be moved.

Benvolio. And what to?

Mercutio. Nay, an there were two such, we should have 15
none shortly, for one would kill the other. Thou!
why, thou wilt quarrel with a man that hath a hair
more or a hair less in his beard than thou hast. Thou
wilt quarrel with a man for cracking nuts, having no
other reason but because thou hast hazel eyes. What 20
eye but such an eye would spy out such a quarrel?
Thy head is as full of quarrels as an egg is full of
meat; and yet thy head hath been beaten as addle as
an egg for quarrelling. Thou hast quarrelled with a
man for coughing in the street, because he hath 25
wakened thy dog that hath lain asleep in the sun.
Didst thou not fall out with a tailor for wearing his

III, i, 8–9 *by the operation . . . drawer* after drinking only two
cups of wine, draws his sword against the waiter 13 *moody* angry
21 *spy out* see occasion for

67

new doublet before Easter? with another for tying his
new shoes with old riband? And yet thou wilt tutor
30 me from quarrelling!

Benvolio. An I were so apt to quarrel as thou art, any
man should buy the fee simple of my life for an hour
and a quarter.

Mercutio. The fee simple? O simple!

Enter Tybalt and others.

35 *Benvolio.* By my head, here come the Capulets.

Mercutio. By my heel, I care not.

Tybalt. Follow me close, for I will speak to them.
Gentlemen, good-den. A word with one of you.

Mercutio. And but one word with one of us?
40 Couple it with something; make it a word and a
blow.

Tybalt. You shall find me apt enough to that, sir, an
you will give me occasion.

Mercutio. Could you not take some occasion without
45 giving?

Tybalt. Mercutio, thou consortest with Romeo.

Mercutio. Consort? What, dost thou make us minstrels? An thou make minstrels of us, look to hear
nothing but discords. Here's my fiddlestick; here's
50 that shall make you dance. Zounds, consort!

Benvolio. We talk here in the public haunt of men.
Either withdraw unto some private place,
Or reason coldly of your grievances,
Or else depart. Here all eyes gaze on us.

Mercutio. Men's eyes were made to look, and let them
55 gaze.
I will not budge for no man's pleasure, I.

---

28 *doublet* jacket 29 *riband* ribbon 32 *fee simple* permanent lease
32–33 *hour and a quarter* probable duration of the lease, i.e. of my
life 34 *O simple* O stupid 38 *good-den* good afternoon 47 *Consort* (1) associate with (2) accompany in vocal or instrumental
music 47–48 *minstrels* a more disreputable title than "musicians"
49 *fiddlestick* i.e. rapier 50 *Zounds* by God's wounds

Enter Romeo.

Tybalt. Well, peace be with you, sir. Here comes my
    man.
Mercutio. But I'll be hanged, sir, if he wear your livery.
    Marry, go before to field, he'll be your follower!
    Your worship in that sense may call him man.   60
Tybalt. Romeo, the love I bear thee can afford
    No better term than this: thou art a villain.
Romeo. Tybalt, the reason that I have to love thee
    Doth much excuse the appertaining rage
    To such a greeting. Villain am I none.   65
    Therefore farewell. I see thou knowest me not.
Tybalt. Boy, this shall not excuse the injuries
    That thou hast done me; therefore turn and draw.
Romeo. I do protest I never injured thee,
    But love thee better than thou canst devise   70
    Till thou shalt know the reason of my love;
    And so, good Capulet, which name I tender
    As dearly as mine own, be satisfied.
Mercutio. O calm, dishonorable, vile submission!
    Alla stoccata carries it away.   *Draws.*   75
    Tybalt, you ratcatcher, will you walk?
Tybalt. What wouldst thou have with me?
Mercutio. Good King of Cats, nothing but one of your
    nine lives. That I mean to make bold withal, and,
    As you shall use me hereafter, dry-beat the rest of the 80
    eight. Will you pluck your sword out of his pilcher
    by the ears? Make haste, lest mine be about your
    ears ere it be out.
Tybalt. I am for you.   *Draws.*
Romeo. Gentle Mercutio, put thy rapier up.   85
Mercutio. Come, sir, your passado!   *They fight.*

58 *livery* servant's uniform ("my man" could mean "my man-
servant")   59 *field* duelling ground   64 *appertaining rage* suitably
angry reaction   70 *devise* understand   72 *tender* value   75 *Alla
stoccata* "at the thrust"; i.e. Tybalt *carries it away* triumphs, gets
away with it   79 *nine lives* proverbial: a cat has nine lives   80
dry-beat thrash   81 *pilcher* scabbard   86 *passado* lunge

Romeo. Draw, Benvolio; beat down their weapons.
Gentlemen, for shame! forbear this outrage!
Tybalt, Mercutio, the Prince expressly hath
90   Forbid this bandying in Verona streets.
Hold, Tybalt! Good Mercutio!
            (*Tybalt under Romeo's arm thrusts Mercutio in,
                        and flies with his Followers.*)
Mercutio.   I am hurt.
A plague a both your houses! I am sped.
Is he gone and hath nothing?
Benvolio.   What, art thou hurt?
Mercutio. Ay, ay, a scratch, a scratch. Marry, 'tis
enough.
95   Where is my page? Go, villain, fetch a surgeon.
                                    Exit Page.
Romeo. Courage, man. The hurt cannot be much.
Mercutio. No, 'tis not so deep as a well, nor so wide as
a church door; but 'tis enough, 'twill serve. Ask for
me tomorrow, and you shall find me a grave man.
100   I am peppered, I warrant, for this world. A plague a
both your houses! Zounds, a dog, a rat, a mouse, a
cat, to scratch a man to death! a braggart, a rogue,
a villain, that fights by the book of arithmetic! Why
the devil came you between us? I was hurt under
105   your arm.
Romeo. I thought all for the best.
Mercutio. Help me into some house, Benvolio,
Or I shall faint. A plague a both your houses!
They have made worms' meat of me. I have it,
110   And soundly too. Your houses!
                        Exit (supported by Benvolio).
Romeo. This gentleman, the Prince's near ally,
My very friend, hath got this mortal hurt

---

92 *a* on   *sped* mortally wounded   99 *grave* (1) serious (2) inhabiting
the grave   103 *by . . . arithmetic* by timing his strokes   109 *worms'
meat* i.e. a corpse   *I have it* I am wounded   112 *very* true

In my behalf — my reputation stained
With Tybalt's slander — Tybalt, that an hour
Hath been my cousin. O sweet Juliet,   115
Thy beauty hath made me effeminate
And in my temper soft'ned valor's steel!

Enter Benvolio.

Benvolio. O Romeo, Romeo, brave Mercutio is dead!
That gallant spirit hath aspired the clouds,
Which too untimely here did scorn the earth.   120
Romeo. This day's black fate on moe days doth
        depend;
This but begins the woe others must end.

Enter Tybalt.

Benvolio. Here comes the furious Tybalt back again.
Romeo. Alive in triumph, and Mercutio slain?
Away to heaven respective lenity,   125
And fire-eyed fury be my conduct now!
Now, Tybalt, take the "villain" back again
That late thou gavest me; for Mercutio's soul
Is but a little way above our heads,
Staying for thine to keep him company.   130
Either thou or I, or both, must go with him.
Tybalt. Thou, wretched boy, that didst consort him here,
Shalt with him hence.
Romeo.   This shall determine that.
                            They fight. Tybalt falls.
Benvolio. Romeo, away, be gone!
The citizens are up, and Tybalt slain.   135
Stand not amazed. The Prince will doom thee death
If thou art taken. Hence, be gone, away!

---

119 *aspired* climbed toward 121 *moe* more *depend* hang down
over 125 *respective lenity* reasoned gentleness (personified as an
angel) 126 *fire-eyed fury* fury personified *conduct* guide

Romeo. O, I am fortune's fool!
Benvolio.   Why dost thou stay?
                                             Exit Romeo.

Enter Citizens.

Citizen. Which way ran he that killed Mercutio?
140   Tybalt, that murderer, which way ran he?
Benvolio. There lies that Tybalt.
Citizen.   Up, sir, go with me.
   I charge thee in the Prince's name obey.

*Enter Prince (attended), old Montague, Capulet, their
   wives, and all.*

Prince. Where are the vile beginners of this fray?
Benvolio. O noble Prince, I can discover all
145   The unlucky manage of this fatal brawl.
   There lies the man, slain by young Romeo,
   That slew thy kinsman, brave Mercutio.
Lady Capulet. Tybalt, my cousin! O my brother's
      child!
   O Prince! O husband! O, the blood is spilled
150   Of my dear kinsman! Prince, as thou art true,
   For blood of ours shed blood of Montague.
   O cousin, cousin!
Prince. Benvolio, who began this bloody fray?
Benvolio. Tybalt, here slain, whom Romeo's hand
      did slay.
155   Romeo, that spoke him fair, bid him bethink
   How nice the quarrel was, and urged withal
   Your high displeasure. All this — utterèd
   With gentle breath, calm look, knees humbly
      bowed —
   Could not take truce with the unruly spleen

138 *fool* dupe, victim   144 *discover* reveal   145 *manage* course   156
nice trivial   159 *spleen* temper

Of Tybalt deaf to peace, but that he tilts   160
With piercing steel at bold Mercutio's breast;
Who, all as hot, turns deadly point to point,
And, with a martial scorn, with one hand beats
Cold death aside and with the other sends
It back to Tybalt, whose dexterity   165
Retorts it. Romeo he cries aloud,
"Hold, friends! friends, part!" and swifter than his
   tongue,
His agile arm beats down their fatal points,
And 'twixt them rushes; underneath whose arm
An envious thrust from Tybalt hit the life   170
Of stout Mercutio, and then Tybalt fled;
But by and by comes back to Romeo,
Who had but newly entertained revenge,
And to't they go like lightning; for, ere I
Could draw to part them, was stout Tybalt slain;   175
And as he fell, did Romeo turn and fly.
This is the truth, or let Benvolio die.

Lady Capulet. He is a kinsman to the Montague;
Affection makes him false, he speaks not true.
Some twenty of them fought in this black strife,   180
And all those twenty could but kill one life.
I beg for justice, which thou, Prince, must give.
Romeo slew Tybalt; Romeo must not live.

Prince. Romeo slew him; he slew Mercutio.
Who now the price of his dear blood doth owe?   185

Montague. Not Romeo, Prince; he was Mercutio's
   friend;
His fault concludes but what the law should end,
The life of Tybalt.

Prince.   And for that offense
Immediately we do exile him hence.
I have an interest in your hate's proceeding,   190
My blood for your rude brawls doth lie a-bleeding;

170 *envious* malicious   173 *entertained* harbored thoughts of

But I'll amerce you with so strong a fine
That you shall all repent the loss of mine.
I will be deaf to pleading and excuses;
195 Nor tears nor prayers shall purchase out abuses.
Therefore use none. Let Romeo hence in haste,
Else, when he is found, that hour is his last.
Bear hence this body, and attend our will.
Mercy but murders, pardoning those that kill.

Exit (with others).

ACT III, SCENE II

Enter Juliet alone.

Juliet. Gallop apace, you fiery-footed steeds,
Towards Phoebus' lodging! Such a wagoner
As Phaëton would whip you to the west
And bring in cloudy night immediately.
5 Spread thy close curtain, love-performing night,
That runaways' eyes may wink, and Romeo
Leap to these arms untalked of and unseen.
Lovers can see to do their amorous rites
By their own beauties; or, if love be blind,
10 It best agrees with night. Come, civil night,
Thou sober-suited matron, all in black,
And learn me how to lose a winning match,
Played for a pair of stainless maidenhoods.
Hood my unmanned blood, bating my cheeks,

---

192 *amerce* penalize 198 *attend our will* come to be judged III, ii,
1 *steeds* horses drawing the chariot of the sun 2 *Phoebus* the sun-
god *lodging* below the western horizon 3 *Phaëton* Phoebus' son,
with whom the horses of the sun ran away 6 *runaways' eyes*
eyes of the sun's horses *wink* close 9 *love* Cupid 14 *Hood* cover
with a hood (falconry) *unmanned* untamed *bating* fluttering

With thy black mantle till strange love grow bold,   15
Think true love acted simple modesty.
Come, night; come, Romeo; come, thou day in
    night;
For thou wilt lie upon the wings of night
Whiter than new snow upon a raven's back.
Come, gentle night; come, loving, black-browed
    night;   20
Give me my Romeo; and, when he shall die,
Take him and cut him out in little stars,
And he will make the face of heaven so fine
That all the world will be in love with night
And pay no worship to the garish sun.   25
O, I have bought the mansion of a love,
But not possessed it; and though I am sold,
Not yet enjoyed. So tedious is this day
As is the night before some festival
To an impatient child that hath new robes   30
And may not wear them. O, here comes my nurse,

Enter Nurse, with cords.

And she brings news; and every tongue that speaks
But Romeo's name speaks heavenly eloquence.
Now, nurse, what news? What hast thou there, the
    cords
That Romeo bid thee fetch?

Nurse.   Ay, ay, the cords.   35
                      (*Throws them down.*)
Juliet. Ay me! what news? Why dost thou wring thy
    hands?
Nurse. Ah, weraday! he's dead, he's dead, he's dead!
We are undone, lady, we are undone!
Alack the day! he's gone, he's killed, he's dead!
Juliet. Can heaven be so envious?

---

15 *strange* unfamiliar   16 *true love acted* the act of true love   37
weraday welladay, alas

40 *Nurse.*   Romeo can,
          Though heaven cannot. O Romeo, Romeo!
          Who ever would have thought it? Romeo!
      Juliet. What devil art thou that dost torment me thus?
          This torture should be roared in dismal hell.
45   Hath Romeo slain himself? Say thou but "I,"
          And that bare vowel "I" shall poison more
          Than the death-darting eye of cockatrice.
          I am not I, if there be such an "I"
          Or those eyes' shot that makes the answer "I."
50   If he be slain, say "I"; or if not, "no."
          Brief sounds determine of my weal or woe.
      Nurse. I saw the wound, I saw it with mine eyes,
          (God save the mark!) here on his manly breast.
          A piteous corse, a bloody piteous corse;
55   Pale, pale as ashes, all bedaubed in blood,
          All in gore-blood. I swounded at the sight.
      Juliet. O, break, my heart! poor bankrout, break at once!
          To prison, eyes; ne'er look on liberty!
          Vile earth, to earth resign; end motion here,
60   And thou and Romeo press one heavy bier!
      Nurse. O Tybalt, Tybalt, the best friend I had!
          O courteous Tybalt! honest gentleman!
          That ever I should live to see thee dead!
      Juliet. What storm is this that blows so contrary?
65   Is Romeo slaught'red, and is Tybalt dead?
          My dearest cousin, and my dearer lord?
          Then, dreadful trumpet, sound the general doom!
          For who is living, if those two are gone?
      Nurse. Tybalt is gone, and Romeo banishèd;
70   Romeo that killed him, he is banishèd.
      Juliet. O God! Did Romeo's hand shed Tybalt's blood?

45–50 *I* with the alternating meaning "ay" 47 *cockatrice* basilisk (a
fabulous serpent which killed with eye-glances) 49 *those eyes' shot*
the Nurse's eye-glance, which may inadvertently reveal her unspoken
answer 53 *God . . . mark* God avert the evil omen 56 *gore-blood*
clotted blood *swounded* swooned 57 *bankrout* bankrupt 59 *Vile
earth* i.e. my body *resign* return 67 *trumpet* i.e. the "last trumpet"
general doom Judgment Day

Nurse. It did, it did! alas the day, it did!

Juliet. O serpent heart, hid with a flow'ring face!
Did ever dragon keep so fair a cave?
Beautiful tyrant; fiend angelical!   75
Dove-feathered raven! wolvish-ravening lamb!
Despisèd substance of divinest show!
Just opposite to what thou justly seem'st —
A damnèd saint, an honorable villain!
O nature, what hadst thou to do in hell   80
When thou didst bower the spirit of a fiend
In mortal paradise of such sweet flesh?
Was ever book containing such vile matter
So fairly bound? O, that deceit should dwell
In such a gorgeous palace!

Nurse.   There's no trust,   85
No faith, no honesty in men; all perjured,
All forsworn, all naught, all dissemblers.
Ah, where's my man? Give me some aqua vitae.
These griefs, these woes, these sorrows make me old.
Shame come to Romeo!

Juliet.   Blistered be thy tongue   90
For such a wish! He was not born to shame.
Upon his brow shame is ashamed to sit;
For 'tis a throne where honor may be crowned
Sole monarch of the universal earth.
O, what a beast was I to chide at him!   95

Nurse. Will you speak well of him that killed your
    cousin?

Juliet. Shall I speak ill of him that is my husband?
Ah, poor my lord, what tongue shall smooth thy
    name
When I, thy three-hours wife, have mangled it?
But wherefore, villain, didst thou kill my cousin?   100

---

73 *flow'ring face* traditionally, the Serpent in Eden appeared to
Eve with the face of a young girl, wreathed in flowers 75 *fiend
angelical* (cf. 2 Corinthians 11:14) 76 *wolvish-ravening lamb*
(cf. Matthew 7:15) 81–82 *spirit . . . paradise* i.e. the Serpent
in Eden 88 *aqua vitae* alcoholic spirits

That villain cousin would have killed my husband.
Back, foolish tears, back to your native spring!
Your tributary drops belong to woe,
Which you, mistaking, offer up to joy.
105 My husband lives, that Tybalt would have slain;
And Tybalt's dead, that would have slain my
        husband.
All this is comfort; wherefore weep I then?
Some word there was, worser than Tybalt's death,
That murd'red me. I would forget it fain;
110 But O, it presses to my memory
Like damnèd guilty deeds to sinners' minds!
"Tybalt is dead, and Romeo — banishèd."
That "banishèd," that one word "banishèd,"
Hath slain ten thousand Tybalts. Tybalt's death
115 Was woe enough, if it had ended there;
Or, if sour woe delights in fellowship
And needly will be ranked with other griefs,
Why followèd not, when she said "Tybalt's dead,"
Thy father, or thy mother, nay, or both,
120 Which modern lamentation might have moved?
But with a rearward following Tybalt's death,
"Romeo is banishèd" — to speak that word
Is father, mother, Tybalt, Romeo, Juliet,
All slain, all dead. "Romeo is banishèd" —
125 There is no end, no limit, measure, bound,
In that word's death; no words can that woe sound.
Where is my father and my mother, nurse?
Nurse. Weeping and wailing over Tybalt's corse.
Will you go to them? I will bring you thither.
Juliet. Wash they his wounds with tears? Mine shall be
130   spent,
When theirs are dry, for Romeo's banishment.
Take up those cords. Poor ropes, you are beguiled,

---

103 *tributary* tribute-paying 117 *needly* necessarily 120 *modern* ordinary, conventional 121 *rearward* rearguard 128 *corse* body

Both you and I, for Romeo is exiled.
He made you for a highway to my bed;
But I, a maid, die maiden-widowèd.   135
Come, cords; come, nurse. I'll to my wedding bed;
And death, not Romeo, take my maidenhead!

Nurse. Hie to your chamber. I'll find Romeo
To comfort you. I wot well where he is.
Hark ye, your Romeo will be here at night.   140
I'll to him; he is hid at Laurence' cell.

Juliet. O, find him! give this ring to my true knight
And bid him come to take his last farewell.

                              Exit (with Nurse).

ACT III, SCENE III

Enter Friar Laurence.

Friar. Romeo, come forth; come forth, thou fearful
    man.
Affliction is enamored of thy parts,
And thou art wedded to calamity.

Enter Romeo.

Romeo. Father, what news? What is the Prince's
    doom?
What sorrow craves acquaintance at my hand   5
That I yet know not?

Friar.   Too familiar
Is my dear son with such sour company.
I bring thee tidings of the Prince's doom.

---

139 *wot* know III, iii, 1 *fearful* full of fear 2 *parts* qualities 8
Prince's doom punishment decreed by the Prince

Romeo. What less than doomsday is the Prince's
    doom?

10 *Friar.* A gentler judgment vanished from his lips —
    Not body's death, but body's banishment.

Romeo. Ha, banishment? Be merciful, say "death";
    For exile hath more terror in his look,
    Much more than death. Do not say "banishment."

15 *Friar.* Hence from Verona art thou banishèd.
    Be patient, for the world is broad and wide.

Romeo. There is no world without Verona walls,
    But purgatory, torture, hell itself.
    Hence banishèd is banished from the world,
20   And world's exile is death. Then "banishèd"
    Is death mistermed. Calling death "banishèd,"
    Thou cut'st my head off with a golden axe
    And smilest upon the stroke that murders me.

Friar. O deadly sin! O rude unthankfulness!
25   Thy fault our law calls death; but the kind Prince,
    Taking thy part, hath rushed aside the law,
    And turned that black word "death" to banishment.
    This is dear mercy, and thou seest it not.

Romeo. 'Tis torture, and not mercy. Heaven is here,
30   Where Juliet lives; and every cat and dog
    And little mouse, every unworthy thing,
    Live here in heaven and may look on her;
    But Romeo may not. More validity,
    More honorable state, more courtship lives
35   In carrion flies than Romeo. They may seize
    On the white wonder of dear Juliet's hand
    And steal immortal blessing from her lips,
    Who, even in pure and vestal modesty,
    Still blush, as thinking their own kisses sin;
40   But Romeo may not, he is banishèd.
    Flies may do this but I from this must fly;
    They are freemen, but I am banishèd.

---

9 *doomsday* i.e. death 10 *vanished* disappeared into air 26
rushed pushed 33 *validity* value 34 *courtship* privilege of wooing
38 *vestal* virgin 39 *kisses* when her lips touch each other

And sayest thou yet that exile is not death?
Hadst thou no poison mixed, no sharp-ground knif
No sudden mean of death, though ne'er so mean,
But "banishèd" to kill me — "banishèd"?
O friar, the damnèd use that word in hell;
Howling attends it! How hast thou the heart,
Being a divine, a ghostly confessor,
A sin-absolver, and my friend professed,   50
To mangle me with that word "banishèd"?

Friar. Thou fond mad man, hear me a little speak.

Romeo. O, thou wilt speak again of banishment.

Friar. I'll give thee armor to keep off that word;
   Adversity's sweet milk, philosophy,   55
   To comfort thee, though thou art banishèd.

Romeo. Yet "banishèd"? Hang up philosophy!
   Unless philosophy can make a Juliet,
   Displant a town, reverse a prince's doom,
   It helps not, it prevails not. Talk no more.   60

Friar. O, then I see that madmen have no ears.

Romeo. How should they, when that wise men have
   no eyes?

Friar. Let me dispute with thee of thy estate.

Romeo. Thou canst not speak of that thou dost not
   feel.
   Wert thou as young as I, Juliet thy love,   65
   An hour but married, Tybalt murderèd,
   Doting like me, and like me banishèd,
   Then mightst thou speak, then mightst thou tear
   thy hair,
   And fall upon the ground, as I do now,
   Taking the measure of an unmade grave.   70
                     Enter Nurse and knock.

Friar. Arise; one knocks. Good Romeo, hide thyself.

Romeo. Not I; unless the breath of heartsick groans
   Mist-like infold me from the search of eyes.
                       (Knock.)

45 *mean . . . mean* means . . . lowly 52 *fond* foolish 63 *dispute* reason *estate* situation 70 *Taking the measure* providing the measurements

Friar. Hark, how they knock! Who's there? Romeo,
arise;

75   Thou wilt be taken. — Stay awhile! — Stand up;
(Knock.)

Run to my study. — By and by! — God's will,
What simpleness is this. — I come, I come!
(Knock.)

Who knocks so hard? Whence come you? What's
your will?

Enter Nurse.

Nurse. Let me come in, and you shall know my errand.
I come from Lady Juliet.

80 *Friar.*   Welcome then.

Nurse. O holy friar, O, tell me, holy friar,
Where is my lady's lord, where's Romeo?

Friar. There on the ground, with his own tears made
drunk.

Nurse. O, he is even in my mistress' case,

85   Just in her case! O woeful sympathy!
Piteous predicament! Even so lies she,
Blubb'ring and weeping, weeping and blubb'ring.
Stand up, stand up! Stand, an you be a man.
For Juliet's sake, for her sake, rise and stand!

90   Why should you fall into so deep an O?

Romeo. (*rises*) Nurse —

Nurse. Ah sir! ah sir! Death's the end of all.

Romeo. Speakest thou of Juliet? How is it with her?
Doth not she think me an old murderer,

95   Now I have stained the childhood of our joy
With blood removed but little from her own?
Where is she? and how doth she! and what says
My concealed lady to our cancelled love?

---

76 *By and by* in a moment   77 *simpleness* stupid conduct   90 *an
O* a fit of groaning   94 *old* hardened   98 *concealed . . . cancelled*
hidden from me . . . invalidated by my act (the two words were
given almost the same pronunciation)

Nurse. O, she says nothing, sir, but weeps and weeps;
   And now falls on her bed, and then starts up,   **100**
   And Tybalt calls; and then on Romeo cries,
   And then down falls again.

Romeo.   As if that name,
   Shot from the deadly level of a gun,
   Did murder her; as that name's cursèd hand
   Murdered her kinsman. O, tell me, friar, tell me,   **105**
   In what vile part of this anatomy
   Doth my name lodge? Tell me, that I may sack
   The hateful mansion.

*(He offers to stab himself, and Nurse snatches the
   dagger away.)*

Friar.   Hold thy desperate hand.
   Art thou a man? Thy form cries out thou art;
   Thy tears are womanish, thy wild acts denote   **110**
   The unreasonable fury of a beast.
   Unseemly woman in a seeming man!
   And ill-beseeming beast in seeming both!
   Thou hast amazed me. By my holy order,
   I thought thy disposition better tempered.   **115**
   Hast thou slain Tybalt? Wilt thou slay thyself?
   And slay thy lady that in thy life lives,
   By doing damnèd hate upon thyself?
   Why railest thou on thy birth, the heaven, and
     earth?
   Since birth and heaven and earth, all three do meet **120**
   In thee at once; which thou at once wouldst lose.
   Fie, fie, thou shamest thy shape, thy love, thy wit,
   Which, like a usurer, abound'st in all,
   And usest none in that true use indeed
   Which should bedeck thy shape, thy love, thy wit. **125**

---

103 *level* aim 106 *anatomy* body 111 *unreasonable* irrational
112 *Unseemly . . . seeming* disorderly . . . apparent 113 *ill-
beseeming . . . both* inappropriate . . . man and woman 120 *all
. . . meet* the soul comes from heaven, the body from earth; they
unite in man at his birth 123 *Which* (you) who *all* all capabilities
124 *true use* proper handling of wealth

Thy noble shape is but a form of wax,
Digressing from the valor of a man;
Thy dear love sworn but hollow perjury,
Killing that love which thou hast vowed to cherish;
130   Thy wit, that ornament to shape and love,
Misshapen in the conduct of them both,
Like powder in a skilless soldier's flask,
Is set afire by thine own ignorance,
And thou dismemb'red with thine own defense.
135   What, rouse thee, man! Thy Juliet is alive,
For whose dear sake thou wast but lately dead.
There art thou happy. Tybalt would kill thee,
But thou slewest Tybalt. There art thou happy too.
The law, that threat'ned death, becomes thy friend
140   And turns it to exile. There art thou happy.
A pack of blessings light upon thy back;
Happiness courts thee in her best array;
But, like a misbehaved and sullen wench,
Thou pout'st upon thy fortune and thy love.
145   Take heed, take heed, for such die miserable.
Go get thee to thy love, as was decreed,
Ascend her chamber, hence and comfort her.
But look thou stay not till the watch be set,
For then thou canst not pass to Mantua,
150   Where thou shalt live till we can find a time
To blaze your marriage, reconcile your friends,
Beg pardon of the Prince, and call thee back
With twenty hundred thousand times more joy
Than thou went'st forth in lamentation.
155   Go before, nurse. Commend me to thy lady,
And bid her hasten all the house to bed,
Which heavy sorrow makes them apt unto.
Romeo is coming.
Nurse. O Lord, I could have stayed here all the night
160   To hear good counsel. O, what learning is!

126 *form of wax* waxwork, outward appearance   130 *wit* intellect
131 *Misshapen* distorted *conduct* guidance   132 *flask* powder horn
134 *defense* i.e. intellect   136 *dead* as one dead   137 *happy* fortunate
151 *blaze* publish

My lord, I'll tell my lady you will come.
Romeo. Do so, and bid my sweet prepare to chide.
Nurse. Here is a ring she bid me give you, sir
  Hie you, make haste, for it grows very late.   *Exit.*
Romeo. How well my comfort is revived by this!   165
Friar. Go hence; good night; and here stands all your
    state:
  Either be gone before the watch be set,
  Or by the break of day disguised from hence.
  Sojourn in Mantua. I'll find out your man,
  And he shall signify from time to time   170
  Every good hap to you that chances here.
  Give me thy hand. 'Tis late. Farewell; good night.
Romeo. But that a joy past joy calls out on me,
  It were a grief so brief to part with thee.
  Farewell.   *Exit.*   175

ACT III, SCENE IV

Enter old Capulet, Lady Capulet, and Paris.

Capulet. Things have fall'n out, sir, so unluckily
  That we have had no time to move our daughter.
  Look you, she loved her kinsman Tybalt dearly,
  And so did I. Well, we were born to die.
  'Tis very late; she'll not come down tonight.   5
  I promise you, but for your comany,
  I would have been abed an hour ago.
Paris. These times of woe afford no times to woo.
  Madam, good night. Commend me to your daughter.
Lady. I will, and know her mind early tomorrow;   10
  Tonight she's mewed up to her heaviness.

166 *here . . . state* here is your situation III, iv, 2 *move* talk
with 11 *mewed up* shut up (falconry) *heaviness* grief

Capulet. Sir Paris, I will make a desperate tender
Of my child's love. I think she will be ruled
In all respects by me; nay more, I doubt it not.
15   Wife, go you to her ere you go to bed;
Acquaint her here of my son Paris' love
And bid her (mark you me?) on Wednesday next —
But soft! what day is this?
Paris.   Monday, my lord.
Capulet. Monday! ha, ha! Well, Wednesday is too
     soon.
20   A Thursday let it be — a Thursday, tell her,
She shall be married to this noble earl.
Will you be ready? Do you like this haste?
We'll keep no great ado — a friend or two;
For hark you, Tybalt being slain so late,
25   It may be thought we held him carelessly,
Being our kinsman, if we revel much
Therefore we'll have some half a dozen friends,
And there an end. But what say you to Thursday?
Paris. My lord, I would that Thursday were tomorrow.
30   *Capulet.* Well, get you gone. A Thursday be it then.
Go you to Juliet ere you go to bed;
Prepare her, wife, against this wedding day.
Farewell, my lord. — Light to my chamber, ho!
Afore me, it is so very very late
35   That we may call it early by and by.
Good night.   *Exit.*

12 *desperate tender* risk-taking offer   20 *A* on   34 *Afore me* a
light oath   35 *by and by* immediately

ACT III, SCENE V

Enter Romeo and Juliet aloft (at the window).

Juliet. Wilt thou be gone? It is not yet near day.
   It was the nightingale, and not the lark,
   That pierced the fearful hollow of thine ear.
   Nightly she sings on yond pomegranate tree.
   Believe me, love, it was the nightingale.   5
Romeo. It was the lark, the herald of the morn;
   No nightingale. Look, love, what envious streaks
   Do lace the severing clouds in yonder East.
   Night's candles are burnt out, and jocund day
   Stands tiptoe on the misty mountain tops.   10
   I must be gone and live, or stay and die.
Juliet. Yond light is not daylight; I know it, I.
   It is some meteor that the sun exhales
   To be to thee this night a torchbearer
   And light thee on thy way to Mantua.   15
   Therefore stay yet; thou need'st not to be gone.
Romeo. Let me be ta'en, let me be put to death.
   I am content, so thou wilt have it so.
   I'll say yon grey is not the morning eye,
   'Tis but the pale reflex of Cynthia's brow;   20
   Nor that is not the lark whose notes do beat
   The vaulty heaven so high above our heads.
   I have more care to stay than will to go.
   Come, death, and welcome! Juliet wills it so.
   How is't, my soul? Let's talk; it is not day.   25
Juliet. It is, it is! Hie hence, be gone, away!
   It is the lark that sings so out of tune,
   Straining harsh discords and unpleasing sharps.
   Some say the lark makes sweet division;
   This doth not so, for she divideth us.   30

III, v, 3 *fearful* apprehensive   9 *Night's candles* the stars   13 *meteor* nocturnal light, such as the will-o'-the-wisp, supposedly of luminous gas given off by the sun or drawn by his power (exhaled) out of marshy ground   20 *reflex . . . brow* reflection of the moon   29 *division* melody

Some say the lark and loathèd toad change eyes;
O, now I would they had changed voices too,
Since arm from arm that voice doth us affray,
Hunting thee hence with hunt's-up to the day.
35 O, now be gone! More light and light it grows.
Romeo. More light and light — more dark and dark
    our woes.

Enter Nurse (hastily).

Nurse. Madam!
Juliet. Nurse?
Nurse. Your lady mother is coming to your chamber.
40 The day is broke; be wary, look about.   *Exit.*
Juliet. Then, window, let day in, and let life out.
Romeo. Farewell, farewell! One kiss, and I'll descend.
                        (*He goes down.*)
Juliet. Art thou gone so, love-lord, ay husband-friend?
    I must hear from thee every day in the hour,
45 For in a minute there are many days.
    O, by this count I shall be much in years
    Ere I again behold my Romeo!
Romeo. Farewell!
    I will omit no opportunity
50 That may convey my greetings, love, to thee.
Juliet. O, think'st thou we shall ever meet again?
Romeo. I doubt it not; and all these woes shall serve
    For sweet discourses in our times to come.
Juliet. O God, I have an ill-divining soul!
55 Methinks I see thee, now thou art so low,
    As one dead in the bottom of a tomb.
    Either my eyesight fails, or thou lookest pale.
Romeo. And trust me, love, in my eye so do you.
    Dry sorrow drinks our blood. Adieu, adieu!   *Exit.*

31 *change* exchange (a folk belief) 33 *affray* frighten 34 *hunt's-up*
morning song to awaken huntsmen 43 *friend* clandestine lover 46
much advanced 54 *ill-divining* prophetic of evil 59 *Dry . . . blood*
the presumed effect of grief was to dry up the blood

Juliet. O Fortune, Fortune! all men call thee fickle.   60
  If thou art fickle, what dost thou with him
  That is renowned for faith? Be fickle, Fortune,
  For then I hope thou wilt not keep him long
  But send him back.
                    (*She goes down from the window.*)

                  Enter Lady Capulet.

Lady. Ho, daughter! are you up?   65
Juliet. Who is't that calls? It is my lady mother.
  Is she not down so late, or up so early?
  What unaccustomed cause procures her hither?
Lady. Why, how now, Juliet?
Juliet.   Madam, I am not well.
Lady. Evermore weeping for your cousin's death?   70
  What, wilt thou wash him from his grave with tears?
  An if thou couldst, thou couldst not make him live.
  Therefore have done. Some grief shows much of
    love;
  But much of grief shows still some want of wit.
Juliet. Yet let me weep for such a feeling loss.   75
Lady. So shall you feel the loss, but not the friend
  Which you weep for.
Juliet.   Feeling so the loss,
  I cannot choose but ever weep the friend.
Lady. Well, girl, thou weep'st not so much for his
    death
  As that the villain lives which slaughtered him.   80
Juliet. What villain, madam?
Lady.   That same villain Romeo.
Juliet. (aside) Villain and he be many miles asunder. —
  God pardon him! I do, with all my heart;
  And yet no man like he doth grieve my heart.
Lady. That is because the traitor murderer lives.   85

67 *down* abed   75 *feeling* deeply felt   84 *like* so much as

Juliet. Ay, madam, from the reach of these my hands.
　　Would none but I might venge my cousin's death!
Lady. We will have vengeance for it, fear thou not.
　　Then weep no more. I'll send to one in Mantua,
90　Where that same banished runagate doth live,
　　Shall give him such an unaccustomed dram
　　That he shall soon keep Tybalt company;
　　And then I hope thou wilt be satisfied.
Juliet. Indeed I never shall be satisfied
95　With Romeo till I behold him — dead —
　　Is my poor heart so for a kinsman vexed.
　　Madam, if you could find out but a man
　　To bear a poison, I would temper it;
　　That Romeo should, upon receipt thereof,
100　Soon sleep in quiet. O, how my heart abhors
　　To hear him named and cannot come to him,
　　To wreak the love I bore my cousin
　　Upon his body that hath slaughtered him!
Lady. Find thou the means, and I'll find such a man.
105　But now I'll tell thee joyful tidings, girl.
Juliet. And joy comes well in such a needy time.
　　What are they, beseech your ladyship?
Lady. Well, well, thou hast a careful father, child;
　　One who, to put thee from thy heaviness,
110　Hath sorted out a sudden day of joy
　　That thou expects not nor I looked not for.
Juliet. Madam, in happy time! What day is that?
Lady. Marry, my child, early next Thursday morn
　　The gallant, young and noble gentleman,
115　The County Paris, at Saint Peter's Church,
　　Shall happily make thee there a joyful bride.
Juliet. Now by Saint Peter's Church, and Peter too,
　　He shall not make me there a joyful bride!
　　I wonder at this haste, that I must wed
120　Ere he that should be husband comes to woo.

---

90 *runagate* renegade 98 *temper* prepare or concoct (with play on
"moderate") 110 *sorted* chosen 112 *in happy time* opportunely

I pray you tell my lord and father, madam,
I will not marry yet; and when I do, I swear
It shall be Romeo, whom you know I hate,
Rather than Paris. These are news indeed!

Lady. Here comes your father. Tell him so yourself,   125
And see how he will take it at your hands.

Enter Capulet and Nurse.

Capulet. When the sun sets the earth doth drizzle dew,
But for the sunset of my brother's son
It rains downright.
How now? a conduit, girl? What, still in tears?   130
Evermore show'ring? In one little body
Thou counterfeit'st a bark, a sea, a wind:
For still thy eyes, which I may call the sea,
Do ebb and flow with tears; the bark thy body is,
Sailing in this salt flood; the winds, thy sighs,   135
Who, raging with thy tears and they with them,
Without a sudden calm will overset
Thy tempest-tossèd body. How now, wife?
Have you deliverèd to her our decree?

Lady. Ay, sir; but she will none, she gives you thanks.   140
I would the fool were married to her grave!

Capulet. Soft! take me with you, take me with you,
wife.
How? Will she none? Doth she not give us thanks?
Is she not proud? Doth she not count her blest,
Unworthy as she is, that we have wrought   145
So worthy a gentleman to be her bride?

Juliet. Not proud you have, but thankful that you
have.
Proud can I never be of what I hate,
But thankful even for hate that is meant love.

---

130 *conduit* water-pipe   137 *sudden* immediate   140 *gives you thanks*
says "No, thank you"   141 *married . . . grave* (a petulant but prophetic comment, like l. 167 below)   142 *take . . . you* let me understand you   145 *wrought* arranged for   146 *bride* bridegroom

Capulet. How, how, how, how, chopped-logic? What is
150   this?
    "Proud" — and "I thank you" — and "I thank you
          not" —
    And yet "not proud"? Mistress minion you,
    Thank me no thankings, nor proud me no prouds,
    But fettle your fine joints 'gainst Thursday next
155   To go with Paris to Saint Peter's Church,
    Or I will drag thee on a hurdle thither.
    Out, you green-sickness carrion! out, you baggage!
    You tallow-face!
Lady.   Fie, fie! what, are you mad?
Juliet. Good father, I beseech you on my knees,
160   Hear me with patience but to speak a word.
Capulet. Hang thee, young baggage! disobedient
          wretch!
    I tell thee what — get thee to church a Thursday
    Or never after look me in the face.
    Speak not, reply not, do not answer me!
165   My fingers itch. Wife, we scarce thought us blest
    That God had lent us but this only child;
    But now I see this one is one too much,
    And that we have a curse in having her.
    Out on her, hilding!
Nurse.   God in heaven bless her!
170   You are to blame, my lord, to rate her so.
Capulet. And why, my Lady Wisdom? Hold your
          tongue,
    Good Prudence. Smatter with your gossips, go!
Nurse. I speak no treason.
Capulet   O, God-i-god-en!
Nurse. May not one speak?

---

150 *chopped-logic* hair-splitting 154 *fettle* prepare 156 *hurdle*
sledge on which criminals were carried to execution 157 *green-
sickness* anaemic *baggage* worthless woman 158 *tallow-face* pale-
face *are you mad* (addressed to Capulet) 162 *a* on 169 *hilding*
worthless creature 170 *rate* scold 172 *Smatter . . . gossips* chatter
with your cronies 173 *God-i-god-en* for God's sake

Capulet.   Peace, you mumbling fool!
  Utter your gravity o'er a gossip's bowl,   175
  For here we need it not.
Lady.   You are too hot.
Capulet. God's bread! it makes me mad.
  Day, night; hour, tide, time; work, play;
  Alone, in company; still my care hath been
  To have her matched; and having now provided   180
  A gentleman of noble parentage,
  Of fair demesnes, youthful, and nobly trained,
  Stuffed, as they say, with honorable parts,
  Proportioned as one's thought would wish a man —
  And then to have a wretched puling fool,   185
  A whining mammet, in her fortune's tender,
  To answer "I'll not wed, I cannot love;
  I am too young, I pray you pardon me"!
  But, an you will not wed, I'll pardon you!
  Graze where you will, you shall not house with me.   190
  Look to't, think on't; I do not use to jest.
  Thursday is near; lay hand on heart, advise:
  An you be mine, I'll give you to my friend;
  An you be not, hang, beg, starve, die in the streets,
  For, by my soul, I'll ne'er acknowledge thee,   195
  Nor what is mine shall never do thee good.
  Trust to't. Bethink you. I'll not be forsworn.   *Exit.*
Juliet. Is there no pity sitting in the clouds
  That sees into the bottom of my grief?
  O sweet my mother, cast me not away!   200
  Delay this marriage for a month, a week;
  Or if you do not, make the bridal bed
  In that dim monument where Tybalt lies.
Lady. Talk not to me, for I'll not speak a word.
  Do as thou wilt, for I have done with thee.   *Exit.*   205

---

177 *bread* bread of the Sacrament 182 *demesnes* domains 185
puling whining 186 *mammet* doll *tender* offer 189 *I'll pardon
you* ironic 191 *do not use* am not accustomed 192 *advise* consider

Juliet. O God! — O nurse, how shall this be prevented?
    My husband is on earth, my faith in heaven.
    How shall that faith return again to earth
    Unless that husband send it me from heaven
210   By leaving earth? Comfort me, counsel me.
    Alack, alack, that heaven should practise stratagems
    Upon so soft a subject as myself! ·
    What say'st thou? Hast thou not a word of joy?
    Some comfort, nurse.
Nurse.   Faith, here it is.
215   Romeo is banished; and all the world to nothing
    That he dares ne'er come back to challenge you;
    Or if he do, it needs must be by stealth.
    Then, since the case so stands as now it doth,
    I think it best you married with the County.
220   O, he's a lovely gentleman!
    Romeo's a dishclout to him. An eagle, madam,
    Hath not so green, so quick, so fair an eye
    As Paris hath. Beshrew my very heart,
    I think you are happy in this second match,
225   For it excels your first; or if it did not,
    Your first is dead — or 'twere as good he were
    As living here and you no use of him.
Juliet. Speak'st thou from thy heart?
Nurse. And from my soul too; else beshrew them both.
230 *Juliet.* Amen!
Nurse. What?
Juliet. Well, thou hast comforted me marvellous much.
    Go in; and tell my lady I am gone,
    Having displeased my father, to Laurence' cell,
235   To make confession and to be absolved.
Nurse. Marry, I will; and this is wisely done.   *Exit.*

---

207 *my faith in heaven* my marriage vow is recorded in heaven
208–210 *How . . . earth* how can I marry unless I am first widowed
215 *all . . . nothing* i.e. it is a safe bet 216 *challenge* demand possession of 221 *dishclout* dishcloth 229 *beshrew* a curse on

Juliet. Ancient damnation! O most wicked fiend!
   Is it more sin to wish me thus forsworn,
   Or to dispraise my lord with that same tongue
   Which she hath praised him with above compare   240
   So many thousand times? Go, counsellor!
   Thou and my bosom henceforth shall be twain.
   I'll to the friar to know his remedy.
   If all else fail, myself have power to die.   *Exit.*

---

237 *Ancient damnation* damnable old woman   242 *bosom* confidence
twain separated

ACT IV, SCENE I

Enter Friar Laurence and County Paris.

Friar. On Thursday, sir? The time is very short.
Paris. My father Capulet will have it so,
    And I am nothing slow to slack his haste.
Friar. You say you do not know the lady's mind.
5   Uneven is the course; I like it not.
Paris. Immoderately she weeps for Tybalt's death,
    And therefore have I little talked of love;
    For Venus smiles not in a house of tears.
    Now, sir, her father counts it dangerous
10   That she do give her sorrow so much sway,
    And in his wisdom hastes our marriage
    To stop the inundation of her tears,
    Which, too much minded by herself alone,
    May be put from her by society.
15   Now do you know the reason of this haste.
Friar. (aside) I would I knew not why it should be
    slowed. —
    Look, sir, here comes the lady toward my cell.

Enter Juliet.

Paris. Happily met, my lady and my wife!
Juliet. That may be, sir, when I may be a wife.
20 *Paris.* That "may be" must be, love, on Thursday next.
Juliet. What must be shall be.
Friar.   That's a certain text.
Paris. Come you to make confession to this father?
Juliet. To answer that, I should confess to you.
Paris. Do not deny to him that you love me.

IV, i, 5 *course* i.e. race course 8 *Venus . . . tears* the influence
of the planet Venus is unfavorable when she appears in the "house"
of a "moist" constellation, such as Pisces or Aquarius; i.e. one
cannot talk of love amidst grief 13 *minded* thought about

Juliet. I will confess to you that I love him.   25
Paris. So will ye, I am sure, that you love me.
Juliet. If I do so, it will be of more price,
  Being spoke behind your back, than to your face.
Paris. Poor soul, thy face is much abused with tears.
Juliet. The tears have got small victory by that,   30
  For it was bad enough before their spite.
Paris. Thou wrong'st it more than tears with that
  report.
Juliet. That is no slander, sir, which is a truth;
  And what I spake, I spake it to my face.
Paris. Thy face is mine, and thou hast sland'red it.   35
Juliet. It may be so, for it is not mine own.
 . Are you at leisure, holy father, now,
  Or shall I come to you at evening mass?
Friar. My leisure serves me, pensive daughter, now.
  My lord, we must entreat the time alone.   40
Paris. God shield I should disturb devotion!
  Juliet, on Thursday early will I rouse ye.
  Till then, adieu, and keep this holy kiss.   *Exit.*
Juliet. O, shut the door! and when thou hast done so,
  Come weep with me — past hope, past cure, past
    help!   45
Friar. Ah, Juliet, I already know thy grief;
  It strains me past the compass of my wits.
  I hear thou must, and nothing may prorogue it,
  On Thursday next be married to this County.
Juliet. Tell me not, friar, that thou hearest of this,   50
  Unless thou tell me how I may prevent it.
  If in thy wisdom thou canst give no help,
  Do thou but call my resolution wise
  And with this knife I'll help it presently.
  God joined my heart and Romeo's, thou our hands;   55
  And ere this hand, by thee to Romeo's sealed,
  Shall be the label to another deed,

41 *shield* forbid 47 *the compass . . . wits* my wits' end 48 *prorogue* postpone 57 *label* i.e. strip of parchment bearing the seal, attached to a deed

Or my true heart with treacherous revolt
Turn to another, this shall slay them both.
60   Therefore, out of thy long-experienced time,
Give me some present counsel; or, behold,
'Twixt my extremes and me this bloody knife
Shall play the umpire, arbitrating that
Which the commission of thy years and art
65   Could to no issue of true honor bring.
Be not so long to speak. I long to die
If what thou speak'st speak not of remedy.
Friar. Hold, daughter. I do spy a kind of hope,
Which craves as desperate an execution
70   As that is desperate which we would prevent.
If, rather than to marry County Paris,
Thou hast the strength of will to slay thyself,
Then is it likely thou wilt undertake
A thing like death to chide away this shame,
75   That cop'st with death himself to scape from it;
And, if thou darest, I'll give thee remedy.
Juliet. O, bid me leap, rather than marry Paris,
From off the battlements of any tower,
Or walk in thievish ways, or bid me lurk
80   Where serpents are; chain me with roaring bears,
Or hide me nightly in a charnel house,
O'ercovered quite with dead men's rattling bones,
With reeky shanks and yellow chapless skulls;
Or bid me go into a new-made grave
85   And hide me with a dead man in his shroud —
Things that, to hear them told, have made me
tremble —
And I will do it without fear or doubt,
To live an unstained wife to my sweet love.
Friar. Hold, then. Go home, be merry, give consent
90   To marry Paris. Wednesday is tomorrow.

---

60 *time* age 62 *extremes* difficulties 64 *commission . . . art* authority of your age and skill 75 *cop'st* encounterest 79 *thievish ways* roads frequented by robbers 81 *charnel house* depository of human bones 83 *reeky* smelly *chapless* jawless

Tomorrow night look that thou lie alone;
Let not the nurse lie with thee in thy chamber.
Take thou this vial, being then in bed,
And this distilling liquor drink thou off;
When presently through all thy veins shall run   95
A cold and drowsy humor; for no pulse
Shall keep his native progress, but surcease;
No warmth, no breath, shall testify thou livest;
The roses in thy lips and cheeks shall fade
To wanny ashes, thy eyes' windows fall   100
Like death when he shuts up the day of life;
Each part, deprived of supple government,
Shall, stiff and stark and cold, appear like death;
And in this borrowèd likeness of shrunk death
Thou shalt continue two-and-forty hours,   105
And then awake as from a pleasant sleep.
Now, when the bridegroom in the morning comes
To rouse thee from thy bed, there art thou dead.
Then, as the manner of our country is,
In thy best robes uncoverèd on the bier   110
Thou shalt be borne to that same ancient vault
Where all the kindred of the Capulets lie.
In the mean time, against thou shalt awake,
Shall Romeo by my letters know our drift;
And hither shall he come; and he and I   115
Will watch thy waking, and that very night
Shall Romeo bear thee hence to Mantua.
And this shall free thee from this present shame,
If no inconstant toy nor womanish fear
Abate thy valor in the acting it.   120
Juliet. Give me, give me! O, tell not me of fear!
Friar. Hold! Get you gone, be strong and prosperous

94 *distilling* infusion **96** *humor* moisture **97** *surcease* cease **100**
wanny pale, shrunken *windows* i.e. eyelids (the figure derives
from the covering of shop-fronts at the close of the day) **102** *supple
government* the life force that keeps the body supple **113** *against
. . . awake* in preparation for your awaking **114** *drift* intention
119 *toy* whim

In this resolve. I'll send a friar with speed
To Mantua, with my letters to thy lord.
Juliet. Love give me strength! and strength shall help
125   afford.
        Farewell, dear father.   *Exit with Friar.*

ACT IV, SCENE II

*Enter Capulet, Lady Capulet, Nurse, and Servingmen,
two or three.*

Capulet. So many guests invite as here are writ.
                                        Exit a Servingman.
        Sirrah, go hire me twenty cunning cooks.
Servingman. You shall have none ill, sir; for I'll try if
        they can lick their fingers.
5   *Capulet.* How canst thou try them so?
Servingman. Marry, sir, 'tis an ill cook that cannot lick
        his own fingers. Therefore he that cannot lick his
        fingers goes not with me.
Capulet. Go, begone.   *Exit Servingman.*
10   We shall be much unfurnished for this time.
        What, is my daughter gone to Friar Laurence?
Nurse. Ay, forsooth.
Capulet. Well, he may chance to do some good on her.
        A peevish self-willed harlotry it is.

Enter Juliet

IV, ii, 5 *try* test   6–7 *'tis . . . fingers* it's a poor cook who doesn't
like to taste the food which he prepares (proverbial)   10 *unfurnished*
unprovided   14 *harlotry* hussy

Nurse. See where she comes from shrift with merry
    look.   15
Capulet. How now, my headstrong? Where have you
    been gadding?
Juliet. Where I have learnt me to repent the sin
    Of disobedient opposition
    To you and your behests, and am enjoined
    By holy Laurence to fall prostrate here   20
    To beg your pardon. Pardon, I beseech you!
    Henceforward I am ever ruled by you.
Capulet. Send for the County. Go tell him of this.
    I'll have this knot knit up tomorrow morning.
Juliet. I met the youthful lord at Laurence' cell   25
    And gave him what becomèd love I might,
    Not stepping o'er the bounds of modesty.
Capulet. Why, I am glad on't. This is well. Stand up.
    This is as't should be. Let me see the County.
    Ay, marry, go, I say, and fetch him hither.   30
    Now, afore God, this reverend holy friar,
    All our whole city is much bound to him.
Juliet. Nurse, will you go with me into my closet
    To help me sort such needful ornaments
    As you think fit to furnish me tomorrow?   35
Lady. No, not till Thursday. There is time enough.
Capulet. Go, nurse, go with her. We'll to church to-
    morrow.   *Exit Juliet and Nurse.*
Lady. We shall be short in our provision.
    'Tis now near night.
Capulet.   Tush, I will stir about,
    And all things shall be well, I warrant thee, wife.   40
    Go thou to Juliet, help to deck up her.
    I'll not to bed tonight; let me alone.
    I'll play the housewife for this once. What, ho!
    They are all forth; well, I will walk myself
    To County Paris, to prepare up him   45

24 *tomorrow morning* i.e. Wednesday, one day earlier than planned
32 *bound* indebted

Against tomorrow. My heart is wondrous light,
Since this same wayward girl is so reclaimed.
Exit with Lady Capulet.

ACT IV, SCENE III

Enter Juliet and Nurse.

Juliet. Ay, those attires are best; but, gentle nurse,
I pray thee leave me to myself tonight;
For I have need of many orisons
To move the heavens to smile upon my state,
5   Which, well thou knowest, is cross and full of sin.

Enter Mother.

Lady. What, are you busy, ho? Need you my help?
Juliet. No, madam; we have culled such necessaries
As are behoveful for our state tomorrow.
So please you, let me now be left alone,
10   And let the nurse this night sit up with you;
For I am sure you have your hands full all
In this so sudden business.
Lady.   Good night.
Get thee to bed, and rest; for thou hast need.
Exit Mother and Nurse.
Juliet. Farewell! God knows when we shall meet again.
15   I have a faint cold fear thrills through my veins
That almost freezes up the heat of life.
I'll call them back again to comfort me.
Nurse! — What should she do here?

IV, iii, 3 *orisons* prayers 5 *cross* perverse 7 *culled* picked out 8
behoveful fitting *state* ceremony 15 *faint* causing faintness

My dismal scene I needs must act alone.
Come, vial.   20
What if this mixture do not work at all?
Shall I be married then tomorrow morning?
No, no! This shall forbid it. Lie thou there.
                              (*Lays down a dagger.*)
What if it be a poison which the friar
Subtly hath minist'red to have me dead,   25
Lest in this marriage he should be dishonored
Because he married me before to Romeo?
I fear it is; and yet methinks it should not,
For he hath still been tried a holy man.
How if, when I am laid into the tomb,   30
I wake before the time that Romeo
Come to redeem me? There's a fearful point!
Shall I not then be stifled in the vault,
To whose foul mouth no healthsome air breathes in,
And there die strangled ere my Romeo comes?   35
Or, if I live, is it not very like
The horrible conceit of death and night,
Together with the terror of the place —
As in a vault, an ancient receptacle
Where for this many hundred years the bones   40
Of all my buried ancestors are packed;
Where bloody Tybalt, yet but green in earth,
Lies fest'ring in his shroud; where, as they say,
At some hours in the night spirits resort —
Alack, alack, is it not like that I,   45
So early waking — what with loathsome smells,
And shrieks like mandrakes torn out of the earth,
That living mortals, hearing them, run mad —
O, if I wake, shall I not be distraught,
Environèd with all these hideous fears,   50
And madly play with my forefathers' joints,

25 *minist'red* administered   29 *tried* proved   37 *conceit* imagination
42 *green* new   45 *like* likely   47 *mandrakes* mandragora (a narcotic
plant with a forked root resembling the human form, supposed to
utter maddening shrieks when uprooted)

And pluck the mangled Tybalt from his shroud,
And, in this rage, with some great kinsman's bone
As with a club dash out my desp'rate brains?
55 O, look! methinks I see cousin's ghost
Seeking out Romeo, that did spit his body
Upon a rapier's point. Stay, Tybalt, stay!
Romeo, I come! this do I drink to thee.
          (*She falls upon her bed within the curtains.*)

ACT IV, SCENE IV

Enter Lady Capulet and Nurse.

Lady. Hold, take these keys and fetch more spices,
    nurse.
Nurse. They call for dates and quinces in the pastry.

Enter old Capulet.

Capulet. Come, stir, stir, stir! The second cock hath
    crowed,
    The curfew bell hath rung, 'tis three o'clock.
5   Look to the baked meats, good Angelica;
    Spare not for cost.
Nurse.   Go, you cot-quean, go,
    Get you to bed! Faith, you'll be sick tomorrow
    For this night's watching.
Capulet. No, not a whit. What, I have watched ere
    now
10 All night for lesser cause, and ne'er been sick.
Lady. Ay, you have been a mouse-hunt in your time;
    But I will watch you from such watching now.
                              Exit Lady and Nurse.
Capulet. A jealous hood, a jealous hood!

IV, iv, 5 *baked meats* meat pies 6 *cot-quean* a man who plays
housewife 8 *watching* staying awake 11. *mouse-hunt* i.e. a nocturnal prowler after women

Enter three or four Fellows with spits and logs and
baskets.

Now, fellow,
What is there?

1. *Fellow.* Things for the cook, sir; but I know not
   what.   15
Capulet. Make haste, make haste. (*Exit first Fellow.*)
   Sirrah, fetch drier logs.
Call Peter; he will show thee where they are.
2. *Fellow.* I have a head, sir, that will find out logs
   And never trouble Peter for the matter.
Capulet. Mass, and well said; a merry whoreson, ha!   20
   Thou shalt be loggerhead. (*Exit second Fellow, with*
   the others.) Good Father 'tis day.
The County will be here with music straight,
For so he said he would.   *Play music.*
                I hear him near.
Nurse! Wife! What, ho! What, nurse, I say!

Enter Nurse.

Go waken Juliet; go and trim her up.   25
I'll go and chat with Paris. Hie, make haste,
Make haste! The bridegroom he is come already:
Make haste, I say.   *Exit.*

ACT IV, SCENE V.

(*Nurse goes to curtains.*)

Nurse. Mistress! what, mistress! Juliet! Fast, I warrant
   her, she.
Why, lamb! why, lady! Fie, you slug-abed.

13 *A jealous hood* you wear the cap (or hood) of jealousy **18** *I
. . . logs* i.e. my head is wooden and has an affinity for logs **20**
Mass by the Mass *whoreson* rascal **21** *loggerhead* blockhead
25 *trim her up* dress her neatly **IV, v, 1** *Fast* fast asleep **2** *slug-
abed* sleepyhead

Why, love, I say! madam! sweetheart! Why, bride!
What, not a word? You take your pennyworths now;
5   Sleep for a week; for the next night, I warrant,
The County Paris hath set up his rest
That you shall rest but little. God forgive me!
Marry, and amen. How sound is she asleep!
I needs must wake her. Madam, madam, madam!
10 Ay, let the County take you in your bed;
He'll fright you up, i' faith. Will it not be?
                    (*Draws aside the curtains.*)
What, dressed, and in your clothes, and down again?
I must needs wake you. Lady! lady! lady!
Alas, alas, Help, help! my lady's dead!
15 O weraday that ever I was born!
Some aqua vitae, ho! My lord! my lady!

                    Enter Lady Capulet.

Lady. What noise is here?
Nurse.   O lamentable day!
Lady. What is the matter?
Nurse.   Look, look! O heavy day!
Lady. O me, O me! My child, my only life!
20 Revive, look up, or I will die with thee!
Help, help! Call help.

                    Enter Capulet.

Capulet. For shame, bring Juliet forth; her lord is
    come.
Nurse. She's dead, deceased; she's dead, alack the day!
Lady. Alack the day, she's dead, she's dead, she's dead!
25 *Capulet.* Ha! let me see her. Out alas! she's cold,
    Her blood is settled, and her joints are stiff;

---

4 *pennyworths* small portions 6 *set . . . rest* i.e. made his firm
decision (from primero, a card game) 12 *down* back to bed 15
weraday welladay, alas 16 *aqua vitae* alcoholic spirits

Life and these lips have long been separated.
Death lies on her like an untimely frost
Upon the sweetest flower of all the field.
Nurse. O lamentable day!
Lady.   O woeful time!   30
Capulet. Death, that hath ta'en her hence to make me
      wail,
Ties up my tongue and will not let me speak.

          *Enter Friar Laurence and the County Paris, with
              Musicians.*

Friar. Come, is the bride ready to go to church?
Capulet. Ready to go, but never to return.
      O son, the night before thy wedding day   35
      Hath Death lain with thy wife. There she lies,
      Flower as she was, deflowerèd by him.
      Death is my son-in-law, Death is my heir;
      My daughter he hath wedded. I will die
      And leave him all. Life, living, all is Death's.   40
Paris. Have I thought long to see this morning's face,
      And doth it give me such a sight as this?
Lady. Accursed, unhappy, wretched, hateful day!
      Most miserable hour that e'er time saw
      In lasting labor of his pilgrimage!   45
      But one, poor one, one poor and loving child,
      But one thing to rejoice and solace in,
      And cruel Death hath catched it from my sight.
Nurse. O woe! O woeful, woeful, woeful day!
      Most lamentable day, most woeful day   50
      That ever ever I did yet behold!
      O day, O day, O day! O hateful day!
      Never was seen so black a day as this.
      O woeful day! O woeful day!

45 *lasting labor* continuous toil

55 *Paris.* Beguiled, divorcèd, wrongèd, spited, slain!
        Most detestable Death, by thee beguiled,
        By cruel cruel thee quite overthrown.
        O love! O life! not life, but love in death!
    Capulet. Despised, distressèd, hated, martyred, killed!
60   Uncomfortable time, why cam'st thou now
        To murder, murder our solemnity?
        O child, O child! my soul, and not my child!
        Dead art thou — alack, my child is dead,
        And with my child my joys are burièd!
65 *Friar.* Peace, ho, for shame! Confusion's cure lives not
        In these confusions. Heaven and yourself
        Had part in this fair maid — now heaven hath all,
        And all the better is it for the maid.
        Your part in her you could not keep from death,
70   But heaven keeps his part in eternal life.
        The most you sought was her promotion,
        For 'twas your heaven she should be advanced;
        And weep ye now, seeing she is advanced
        Above the clouds, as high as heaven itself?
75   O, in this love, you love your child so ill
        That you run mad, seeing that she is well.
        She's not well married that lives married long,
        But she's best married that dies married young.
        Dry up your tears and stick your rosemary
80   On this fair corse, and, as the custom is,
        In all her best array bear her to church;
        For though fond nature bids us all lament,
        Yet nature's tears are reason's merriment.
    Capulet. All things that we ordainèd festival
85   Turn from their office to black funeral —
        Our instruments to melancholy bells,
        Our wedding cheer to a sad burial feast;

61 *To murder . . . solemnity* to spoil our ceremony 69 *Your part*
her mortal body, generated by her parents 70 *his part* her
immortal soul, created directly by God 79 *rosemary* plant symboliz-
ing remembrance 82 *fond nature* foolish human nature 83 *merri-
ment* cause for optimism

Our solemn hymns to sullen dirges change;
Our bridal flowers serve for a buried corse;
And all things change them to the contrary.   90
Friar. Sir, go you in; and madam, go with him;
And go, Sir Paris. Every one prepare
To follow this fair corse unto her grave.
The heavens do low'r upon you for some ill;
Move them no more by crossing their high will.   95
　　*Exit (casting rosemary on her and shutting the
　　curtain).*

　　　　　　　　　　The Nurse and Musicians Remain.

1. *Musician.* Faith, we may put up our pipes and be
　gone.
Nurse. Honest good fellows, ah, put up, put up!
　For well you know this is a pitiful case.   *Exit.*
1. *Musician.* Ay by my troth, the case may be amended.

　　　　　　　　　　Enter Peter.

Peter. Musicians, O, musicians, "Heart's ease,"   100
　"Heart's ease"! O, an you will have me live, play
　"Heart's ease."
1. *Musician.* Why "Heart's ease"?
Peter. O, musicians, because my heart itself plays
　"My heart is full of woe." O, play me some merry   105
　dump to comfort me.
1. *Musician.* Not a dump we! 'Tis no time to play now.
Peter. You will not then?
1. *Musician.* No.
Peter. I will then give it you soundly.   110
1. *Musician.* What will you give us?
Peter. No money, on my faith, but the gleek. I will give
　you the minstrel.
1. *Musician.* Then will I give you the the serving-
　creature.   115

---

94 *low'r* look angrily *ill* sin 99 *case* instrument case *amended*
repaired 100–103 *Heart's ease, My heart is full of woe* old ballad
tunes 104 *dump* slow dance melody

Peter. Then will I lay the serving-creature's dagger on
your pate. I will carry no crotchets. I'll re you, I'll
fa you. Do you note me?

1. *Musician.* An you re us and fa us, you note us.

120 2. *Musician.* Pray you put up your dagger, and put out
your wit.

Peter. Then have at you with my wit! I will dry-beat
you with an iron wit, and put up my iron dagger.
Answer me like men.

125   "When griping grief the heart doth wound,
                and doleful dumps the mind oppress,
            Then music with her silver sound" —
Why "silver sound"? Why "music with her silver
sound"?

130 What say you, Simon Catling?

1. *Musician.* Marry, sir, because silver hath a sweet
sound.

Peter. Pretty! What say you, Hugh Rebeck?

2. *Musician.* I say "silver sound" because musicians
135 sound for silver.

Peter. Pretty too! What say you, James Soundpost?

3. *Musician.* Faith, I know not what to say.

Peter. O, I cry you mercy! you are the singer. I will say
for you. It is "music with her silver sound" because
140 musicians have no gold for sounding.
            "Then music with her silver sound
                With speedy help doth lend redress."   *Exit.*

1. *Musician.* What a pestilent knave is this same!

2. *Musician.* Hang him, Jack! Come, we'll in here,
145 tarry for the mourners, and stay dinner.

                                    Exit with others.

---

112 *gleek* mock **112–113** *give you* insultingly call you **117** *carry
put up with crotchets* (1) whims (2) quarter notes in music **117–
118** *re, fa* musical notes **120** *put out* display **122** *dry-beat* thrash
125–127 The song is from Richard Edwards' "In Commendation of
Music," in *The Paradise of Dainty Devices,* 1576. **130** *Catling*
lutestring **133** *Rebeck* three-stringed fiddle **136** *Soundpost* wooden
peg in a violin, supporting the bridge **138** *cry you mercy* beg your
pardon **145** *stay* await

Enter Romeo's Man, Balthasar.

Enter Romeo.

Romeo. If I may trust the flattering truth of sleep,
  My dreams presage some joyful news at hand.
  My bosom's lord sits lightly in his throne,
  And all this day an unaccustomed spirit
  Lifts me above the ground with cheerful thoughts.   5
  I dreamt my lady came and found me dead
  (Strange dream that gives a dead man leave to
     think!)
  And breathed such life with kisses in my lips
  That I revived and was an emperor.
  Ah me! how sweet is love itself possessed,   10
  When but love's shadows are so rich in joy!

Enter Romeo's Man, Balthasar.

  News from Verona! How now, Balthasar?
  Dost thou not bring me letters from the friar?
  How doth my lady? is my father well?
  How fares my Juliet? That I ask again,   15
  For nothing can be ill if she be well.
Man. Then she is well, and nothing can be ill.
  Her body sleeps in Capel's monument,
  And her immortal part with angels lives.
  I saw her laid low in her kindred's vault   20
  And presently took post to tell it you.
  O, pardon me for bringing these ill news,
  Since you did leave it for my office, sir.

V, i, 1 *flattering* favorable to me 3 *bosom's lord* heart 11 *shadows*
dream-images 21 *presently* at once *took post* hired posthorses

Romeo. Is it e'en so? Then I defy you, stars!
25   Thou knowest my lodging. Get me ink and paper
And hire posthorses. I will hence tonight.
Man. I do beseech you, sir, have patience.
Your looks are pale and wild and do import
Some misadventure.
30   *Romeo.*   Tush, thou are deceived.
Leave me and do the thing I bid thee do.
Hast thou no letters to me from the friar?
Man. No, my good lord.
Romeo.   No matter. Get thee gone
And hire those horses. I'll be with thee straight.
                                        Exit Balthasar.
Well, Juliet, I will lie with thee tonight.
35   Let's see for means. O mischief, thou art swift.
To enter in the thoughts of desperate men!
I do remember an apothecary,
And hereabouts 'a dwells, which late I noted
In tatt'red weeds, with overwhelming brows,
40   Culling of simples. Meagre were his looks,
Sharp misery had worn him to the bones;
And in his needy shop a tortoise hung,
An alligator stuffed, and other skins
Of ill-shaped fishes; and about his shelves
45   A beggarly account of empty boxes,
Green earthen pots, bladders, and musty seeds,
Remnants of packthread, and old cakes of roses
Were thinly scattered, to make up a show.
Noting this penury, to myself I said,
50   "An if a man did need a poison now
Whose sale is present death in Mantua,
Here lives a caitiff wretch would sell it him."
O, this same thought did but forerun my need,

---

28 *import* suggest   39 *weeds* garments   *overwhelming* overhanging
40 *simples* herbs   45 *account* quantity   47 *cakes of roses* compressed
rose petals, used for perfume   52 *caitiff* miserable

And this same needy man must sell it me.
As I remember, this should be the house.   55
Being holiday, the beggar's shop is shut.
What, ho! apothecary!

Enter Apothecary.

Apothecary.   Who calls so loud?
Romeo. Come hither, man. I see that thou art poor.
Hold, there is forty ducats. Let me have
A dram of poison, such soon-speeding gear   60
As will disperse itself through all the veins
That the life-weary taker may fall dead,
And that the trunk may be discharged of breath
As violently as hasty powder fired
Doth hurry from the fatal cannon's womb.   65
Apothecary. Such mortal drugs I have; but Mantua's
law is death to any he that utters them.
Romeo. Art thou so bare and full of wretchedness
And fearest to die? Famine is in thy cheeks,
Need and oppression starveth in thy eyes,   70
Contempt and beggary hangs upon thy back:
The world is not thy friend, nor the world's law;
The world affords no law to make thee rich;
Then be not poor, but break it and take this.
Apothecary. My poverty but not my will consents.   75
Romeo. I pay thy poverty and not thy will.
Apothecary. Put this in any liquid thing you will
And drink it off, and if you had the strength
Of twenty men, it would dispatch you straight.
Romeo. There is thy gold — worse poison to men's
souls.   8c
Doing more murder in this loathsome world,
Than these poor compounds that thou mayst not
sell.

60 *gear* stuff 65 *womb* i.e. barrel 66 *mortal* deadly 67 *utters*
gives out 70 *starveth* are revealed by the starved look

I sell thee poison; thou hast sold me none.
Farewell. Buy food and get thyself in flesh.
85 Come, cordial and not poison, go with me
To Juliet's grave; for there must I use thee.   *Exit.*

ACT V, SCENE II

Enter Friar John to Friar Laurence.

John. Holy Franciscan friar, brother; ho!

Enter Friar Laurence.

Laurence. This same should be the voice of Friar John.
Welcome from Mantua. What says Romeo?
Or, if his mind be writ, give me his letter.
5 *John.* Going to find a barefoot brother out,
One of our order, to associate me
Here in this city visiting the sick,
And finding him, the searchers of the town,
Suspecting that we both were in a house
10 Where the infectious pestilence did reign,
Sealed up the doors, and would not let us forth,
So that my speed to Mantua there was stayed.
Laurence. Who bare my letter, then, to Romeo?
John. I could not send it — here it is again —
15 Nor get a message to bring it thee,
So fearful were they of infection.
Laurence. Unhappy fortune! By my brotherhood,
The letter was not nice, but full of charge,

V, ii, 5 *a barefoot brother* another friar 6 *associate* accompany
8 *searchers* health officers 10 *pestilence* plague 17 *brotherhood* order
(Franciscans) 18 *nice* trivial *charge* important matters

Of dear import; and the neglecting it
May do much danger. Friar John, go hence,   20
Get me an iron crow and bring it straight
Unto my cell.

John.   Brother, I'll go and bring it thee.   *Exit.*
Laurence. Now must I to the monument alone.
Within this three hours will fair Juliet wake.
She will beshrew me much that Romeo   25
Hath had no notice of these accidents;
But I will write again to Mantua,
And keep her at my cell till Romeo come —
Poor living corse, closed in a dead man's tomb! *Exit.*

ACT V, SCENE III

Enter Paris and his Page (with flowers and sweet water).

Paris. Give me thy torch, boy. Hence, and stand aloof.
Yet put it out, for I would not be seen.
Under yond yew tree lay thee all along,
Holding thy ear close to the hollow ground.
So shall no foot upon the churchyard tread   5
(Being loose, unfirm, with digging up of graves)
But thou shalt hear it. Whistle then to me,
As signal that thou hearest something approach.
Give me those flowers. Do as I bid thee, go.
Page. (aside) I am almost afraid to stand alone   10
Here in the churchyard; yet I will adventure.
                                        Retires.

21 *crow* crowbar   25 *beshrew* reprove   26 *accidents* occurrences
V, iii, 3 *all along* at full length

Paris. Sweet flower, with flowers thy bridal bed I strew
(O woe! thy canopy is dust and stones)
Which with sweet water nightly I will dew;
15 Or, wanting that, with tears distilled by moans.
The obsequies that I for thee will keep
Nightly shall be to strew thy grave and weep.

Whistle Boy.

The boy gives warning something doth approach.
What cursèd foot wanders this way tonight
20 To cross my obsequies and true love's rite?
What, with a torch? Muffle me, night, awhile.

Retires.

*Enter Romeo, and Balthasar with a torch, a mattock,
and a crow of iron.*

Romeo. Give me that mattock and the wrenching iron.
Hold, take this letter. Early in the morning
See thou deliver it to my lord and father.
25 Give me the light. Upon thy life I charge thee,
Whate'er thou hearest or seest, stand all aloof
And do not interrupt me in my course.
Why I descend into this bed of death
Is partly to behold my lady's face,
30 But chiefly to take thence from her dead finger
A precious ring — a ring that I must use
In dear employment. Therefore hence, be gone.
But if thou, jealous, dost return to pry
In what I farther shall intend to do,
35 By heaven, I will tear thee joint by joint
And strew this hungry churchyard with thy limbs.
The time and my intents are savage-wild,
More fierce and more inexorable far
Than empty tigers or the roaring sea.

---

20 *cross* interfere with 22 *mattock* pickaxe 31 *A precious ring*
a false excuse to assure Balthasar's noninterference 33 *jealous*
curious, jealous of my privacy

Balthasar. I will be gone, sir, and not trouble you.   40
Romeo. So shalt thou show me friendship. Take thou
    that. Live, and be prosperous; and farewell, good
    fellow.

Balthasar. (aside) For all this same, I'll hide me here-
    about. His looks I fear, and his intents I doubt.
                                Retires.
Romeo. Thou detestable maw, thou womb of death,   45
    Gorged with the dearest morsel of the earth,
    Thus I enforce thy rotten jaws to open,
    And in despite I'll cram thee with more food.
                (Romeo opens the tomb.)
Paris. This is that banished haughty Montague
    That murd'red my love's cousin — with which grief   50
    It is supposèd the fair creature died —
    And here is come to do some villainous shame
    To the dead bodies. I will apprehend him.
    Stop thy unhallowèd toil, vile Montague!
    Can vengeance be pursued further than death?   55
    Condemnèd villain, I do apprehend thee.
    Obey, and go with me; for thou must die.
Romeo. I must indeed; and therefore came I hither.
    Good gentle youth, tempt not a desp'rate man.
    Fly hence and leave me. Think upon these gone;   60
    Let them affright thee. I beseech thee, youth,
    Put not another sin upon my head
    By urging me to fury. O, be gone!
    By heaven, I love thee better than myself,
    For I come hither armed against myself.   65
    Stay not, be gone. Live, and hereafter say
    A madman's mercy bid thee run away.
Paris. I do defy thy conjuration
    And apprehend thee for a felon here.
Romeo. Wilt thou provoke me? Then have at thee,
    boy!   *(They fight.)*   70

---

42 *that* a purse   48 *in despite* to spite you   53 *apprehend* arrest   60
gone dead   68 *conjuration* threatening appeal

Page. O Lord, they fight! I will go call the watch.

> *Exit. Paris falls.*

Paris. O, I am slain! If thou be merciful,
  Open the tomb, lay me with Juliet.   *(Dies.)*

Romeo. In faith, I will. Let me peruse this face.
75   Mercutio's kinsman, noble County Paris!
  What said my man when my betossèd soul
  Did not attend him as we rode? I think
  He told me Paris should have married Juliet.
  Said he not so? or did I dream it so?
80   Or am I mad, hearing him talk of Juliet,
  To think it was so? O, give me thy hand,
  One writ with me in sour misfortune's book!
  I'll bury thee in a triumphant grave.
  A grave? O, no, a lanthorn, slaught'red youth,
85   For here lies Juliet, and her beauty makes
  This vault a feasting presence full of light.
  Death, lie thou there, by a dead man interred.

> *(Lays him in the tomb.)*

  How oft when men are at the point of death
  Have they been merry! which their keepers call
90   A lightning before death. O, how may I
  Call this a lightning? O my love; my wife!
  Death, that hath sucked the honey of thy breath,
  Hath had no power yet upon thy beauty.
  Thou art not conquered. Beauty's ensign yet
95   Is crimson in thy lips and in thy cheeks,
  And death's pale flag is not advancèd there.
  Tybalt, liest thou there in thy bloody sheet?
  O, what more favor can I do to thee
  Than with that hand that cut thy youth in twain
100   To sunder his that was thine enemy?
  Forgive me, cousin! Ah, dear Juliet,

---

74 *peruse* read, look at 77 *attend* pay attention to 84 *lanthorn* lantern (a many-windowed turret room) 86 *presence* presence chamber 89 *keepers* jailers 90 *A lightning before death* a common phrase for the phenomenon described 94 *ensign* banner

Why art thou yet so fair? Shall I believe
That unsubstantial Death is amorous,
And that the lean abhorrèd monster keeps
Thee here in dark to be his paramour?   105
For fear of that I still will stay with thee
And never from this pallet of dim night
Depart again. Here, here will I remain
With worms that are thy chambermaids. O, here
Will I set up my everlasting rest   110
And shake the yoke of inauspicious stars
From this world-wearied flesh. Eyes, look your last!
Arms, take your last embrace! and, lips, O you
The doors of breath, seal with a righteous kiss
A dateless bargain to engrossing death!   115
Come, bitter conduct; come, unsavory guide!
Thou desperate pilot, now at once run on
The dashing rocks thy seasick weary bark!
Here's to my love! (*Drinks.*) O true apothecary!
Thy drugs are quick. Thus with a kiss I die.   120
                                    (*Falls.*)

Enter Friar Laurence, with lanthorn, crow, and spade.

Friar. Saint Francis be my speed! how oft tonight
    Have my old feet stumbled at graves! Who's there?
Balthasar. Here's one, a friend, and one that knows you
    well.
Friar. Bliss be upon you! Tell me, good my friend,
    What torch is yond that vainly lends his light   125
    To tombs and eyeless skulls? As I discern,
    It burneth in the Capels' monument.
Balthasar. It doth so, holy sir; and there's my master,
    One that you love.

110 *set . . . rest* make my decision to stay forever 115 *dateless* in
perpetuity *engrossing* taking everything 116 *conduct* guide, i.e.
the poison 117 *pilot* i.e. Romeo's soul 118 *bark* i.e. Romeo's
body 121 *speed* aid 122 *stumbled at graves* a bad omen

Friar.   Who is it?
Balthasar.   Romeo.
Friar. How long hath he been there?
130 *Balthasar.*   Full half an hour.
.*Friar.* Go with me to the vault.
Balthasar.   I dare not, sir.
    My master knows not but I am gone hence,
    And fearfully did menace me with death
    If I did stay to look on his intents.
135 *Friar.* Stay then; I'll go alone. Fear comes upon me.
    O, much I fear some ill unthrifty thing.
    Balthasar. As I did sleep under this yew tree here,
    I dreamt my master and another fought,
    And that my master slew him.
    Friar.   Romeo!
140 Alack, alack, what blood is this which stains
    The stony entrance of this sepulchre?
    What mean these masterless and gory swords
    To lie discolored by this place of peace?
                            (*Enters the tomb.*)
    Romeo! O, pale! Who else? What, Paris too?
145 And steeped in blood? Ah, what an unkind hour
    Is guilty of this lamentable chance!
    The lady stirs.   (*Juliet rises.*)
Juliet. O comfortable friar! where is my lord?
    I do remember well where I should be,
150 And there I am. Where is my Romeo?
Friar. I hear some noise. Lady, come from that nest
    Of death, contagion, and unnatural sleep.
    A greater power than we can contradict
    Hath thwarted our intents. Come, come away.
155 Thy husband in thy bosom there lies dead;
    And Paris too. Come, I'll dispose of thee
    Among a sisterhood of holy nuns.

136 *unthrifty* unfortunate   148 *comfortable* comfort-giving

Stay not to question, for the watch is coming.
Come, go, good Juliet. I dare no longer stay.
Juliet. Go, get thee hence, for I will not away.   160
                                Exit Friar.
What's here? A cup, closed in my true love's hand?
Poison, I see, hath been his timeless end.
O churl! drunk all, and left no friendly drop
To help me after? I will kiss thy lips.
Haply some poison yet doth hang on them   165
To make me die with a restorative.   (*Kisses him.*)
Thy lips are warm!
Chief Watchman. (*within*) Lead, boy. Which way?
Juliet. Yea, noise? Then I'll be brief. O happy dagger!
                   (*Snatches Romeo's dagger.*)
This is thy sheath; there rust, and let me die.   170
                (*She stabs herself and falls.*)

         Enter Paris's Boy and Watch.

Boy. This is the place. There, where the torch doth burn.
Chief Watchman. The ground is bloody. Search about the churchyard.
Go, some of you; whoe'er you find attach.
                    Exit some of the Watch.
Pitiful sight! here lies the County slain;
And Juliet bleeding, warm, and newly dead,   175
Who here hath lain this two days burièd.
Go, tell the Prince; run to the Capulets;
Raise up the Montagues; some others search.
                    Exit others of the Watch.
We see the ground whereon these woes do lie,
But the true ground of all these piteous woes   180
We cannot without circumstance descry.

---

162 *timeless* untimely   166 *restorative* i.e. restoring me to you   169
happy opportune   180 *ground* basis   181 *circumstance* details

Enter some of the Watch, with Romeo's Man Balthasar.

2. *Watchman.* Here's Romeo's man. We found him
in the churchyard.
Chief Watchman. Hold him in safety till the Prince
come hither.

Enter Friar Laurence and another Watchman.

3. *Watchman.* Here is a friar that trembles, sighs, and
weeps.
   We took this mattock and this spade from
185   him
   As he was coming from this churchyard side.
Chief Watchman. A great suspicion! Stay the friar too.

Enter the Prince and Attendants.

Prince. What misadventure is so early up,
   That calls our person from our morning rest?

Enter Capulet and his Lady with others.

Capulet. What should it be, that is so shrieked
190   abroad?
Lady. O, the people in the street cry "Romeo,"
   Some "Juliet," and some "Paris"; and all run,
   With open outcry, toward our monument.
Prince. What fear is this which startles in your ears?
Chief Watchman. Sovereign, here lies the County
195   Paris slain;
   And Romeo dead; and Juliet, dead before,
   Warm and new killed.
Prince. Search, seek, and know how this foul murder
   comes.
Chief Watchman. Here is a friar, and slaughtered
   Romeo's man,

With instruments upon them fit to open.   200
These dead men's tombs.

Capulet. O heavens! O wife, look how our daughter
   bleeds!
  This dagger hath mista'en, for lo, his house
  Is empty on the back of Montague,
  And it missheathèd in my daughter's bosom!   205

Lady. O me! this sight of death is as a bell
  That warns my old age to a sepulchre.

Enter Montague and others.

Prince. Come, Montague; for thou art early up
  To see thy son and heir more early down.

Montague. Alas, my liege, my wife is dead tonight!   210
  Grief of my son's exile hath stopped her breath.
  What further woe conspires against mine age?

Prince. Look, and thou shalt see.

Montague. O thou untaught! what manners is in this,
  To press before thy father to a grave?   215

Prince. Seal up the mouth of outrage for a while,
  Till we can clear these ambiguities
  And know their spring, their head, their true descent;
  And then will I be general of your woes
  And lead you even to death. Meantime forbear,   220
  And let mischance be slave to patience.
  Bring forth the parties of suspicion.

Friar. I am the greatest, able to do least,
  Yet most suspected, as the time and place
  Doth make against me, of this direful murder;   225
  And here I stand, both to impeach and purge
  Myself condemnèd and myself excused.

Prince. Then say at once what thou dost know in this.

---

203 *his house* its sheath   207 *my old age* she is only twenty-eight but
she feels old and ready for death   216 *mouth of outrage* violent
outcries   219 *general . . . woes* your leader in lamentation   220
even to death even if grief kills us   226 *impeach and purge* accuse
and exonerate

Friar. I will be brief, for my short date of breath
230   Is not so long as is a tedious tale.
Romeo, there dead, was husband to that Juliet;
And she, there dead, that Romeo's faithful wife.
I married them; and their stol'n marriage day
Was Tybalt's doomsday, whose untimely death
235   Banished the new-made bridegroom from this city;
For whom, and not for Tybalt, Juliet pined.
You, to remove that siege of grief from her,
Betrothed and would have married her perforce
To County Paris. Then comes she to me
240   And with wild looks bid me devise some mean
To rid her from this second marriage,
Or in my cell there would she kill herself.
Then gave I her (so tutored by my art)
A sleeping potion; which so took effect
245   As I intended, for it wrought on her
The form of death. Meantime I writ to Romeo
That he should hither come as this dire night
To help to take her from her borrowèd grave,
Being the time the potion's force should cease.
250   But he which bore my letter, Friar John,
Was stayed by accident, and yesternight
Returned my letter back. Then all alone
At the prefixèd hour of her waking
Came I to take her from her kindred's vault;
255   Meaning to keep her closely at my cell
Till I conveniently could send to Romeo.
But when I came, some minute ere the time
Of her awakening, here untimely lay
The noble Paris and true Romeo dead.
260   She wakes; and I entreated her come forth
And bear this work of heaven with patience;
But then a noise did scare me from the tomb,

---

229 *date of breath* life expectancy 238 *perforce* by force 247 *as*
on 255 *closely* secretly

And she, too desperate, would not go with me,
But, as it seems, did violence on herself.
All this I know, and to the marriage   265
Her nurse is privy; and if aught in this
Miscarried by my fault, let my old life
Be sacrificed, some hour before his time,
Unto the rigor of severest law.

Prince. We still have known thee for a holy man.   270
Where's Romeo's man? What can he say in this?

Balthasar. I brought my master news of Juliet's death;
And then in post he came from Mantua
To this same place, to this same monument.
This letter he early bid me give his father,   275
And threat'ned me with death, going in the vault,
If I departed not and left him there.

Prince. Give me the letter. I will look on it.
Where is the County's page that raised the watch?
Sirrah, what made your master in this place?   280

Boy. He came with flowers to strew his lady's grave;
And bid me stand aloof, and so I did.
Anon comes one with light to ope the tomb;
And by and by my master drew on him;
And then I ran away to call the watch.   285

Prince. This letter doth make good the friar's words,
Their course of love, the tidings of her death;
And here he writes that he did buy a poison
Of a poor apothecary, and therewithal
Came to this vault to die, and lie with Juliet.   290
Where be these enemies? Capulet, Montague,
See what a scourge is laid upon your hate,
That heaven finds means to kill your joys with love.
And I, for winking at your discords too,
Have lost a brace of kinsmen. All are punished.   295

---

266 *privy* in the secret 270 *still* always 280 *made* did 283 *Anon*
soon 284 *by and by* almost at once *drew* drew his sword 293 *with*
by means of 294 *winking at* shutting my eyes to

Capulet. O brother Montague, give me thy hand
  This is my daughter's jointure, for no more
  Can I demand.

Montague.   But I can give thee more;
  For I will raise her statue in pure gold,
300   That while Verona by that name is known,
  There shall no figure at such rate be set
  As that of true and faithful Juliet.

Capulet. As rich shall Romeo's by his lady lie —
  Poor sacrifices of our enmity!

305 *Prince.* A glooming peace this morning with it brings.
  The sun for sorrow will not show his head.
  Go hence, to have more talk of these sad things;
  Some shall be pardoned, and some punishèd;
  For never was a story of more woe
310   Than this of Juliet and her Romeo.   *Exit all.*